A Seasoning of Menus

GEORGINA INFIELD

Illustrated by
FAITH JAQUES

HEINEMANN : LONDON

William Heinemann Ltd
London Melbourne Toronto
Johannesburg Auckland

First Published 1969
© Georgina Infield 1969

434 94320 7

Made and Printed in Great Britain by
Morrison and Gibb Ltd, London and Edinburgh

Contents

Introduction   vii

SPECIAL OCCASIONS   1

SUMMER DINNERS   9

WINTER DINNERS   41

SUMMER LUNCHEONS
     AND FAMILY SUPPERS   73

WINTER LUNCHEONS
     AND FAMILY SUPPERS   105

BASIC RECIPES   137

GLOSSARY   140

Index   143

Introduction

This book is divided into menus instead of the more usual chapters. This seems to me to be a more sensible method of division as it is easier to select a whole menu at a glance instead of sorting out the recipes one by one.

After each menu you will find a shopping list for the more important items. I have tried to arrange these in order of shops; for example, the food to be bought from the butcher or the fishmonger will come at the top of the list, then all the things to be bought from the greengrocer will come next, and so on. I have presumed in most cases that you will have normal stores of salt, pepper, oil, vinegar, flour, bread, garlic, assorted spices, etc., and a reasonable quantity of milk, butter, eggs, and sugar (granulated, caster, and Demerara); but if any extra supplies of these things or rather unusual spices are required, I have included these in the shopping lists. Of course, it is up to you to make *quite* sure that you have everything you will need for the recipes and the lists are only intended as a general guide.

Though not specified in the recipes, you will find that sea salt, fresh ground black pepper, wine vinegar, and unsalted butter will give the best results. At the back of the book you will find recipes for French dressing, sweet French dressing, mayonnaise, béchamel sauce, and vanilla sugar.

There are menus suitable for dinners, luncheons, family suppers, and two special party menus.

The dinners are suitable for medium formal entertaining of the type that most people find quite adequate for their needs in these days of no domestic help, expensive food, and wives going out to work.

Most of the meals can be prepared almost entirely in advance; indeed in many cases it is advisable, for certain foods taste better if they are allowed to rest for a day and then reheated. There is nothing forbiddingly *haute cuisine* in these menus although some

vii

of them are naturally more expensive than others; but you cannot expect to eat well and entertain without spending some money sometimes! They are, of course, quite suitable for family meals if you have the time, cash, and capacity.

I have divided the menus into winter and summer only, as spring and autumn seem to run together with the other seasons both as regards weather and seasonal food. It will be noticed that in most cases I have not suggested serving a hot vegetable, for two reasons. The first is a practical one: vegetables have to be very well cooked indeed to be palatable and if you want to spend time with your guests, as I do, then you cannot be in the kitchen watching the pot. Also most vegetables smell extremely nasty while they are cooking and nothing is more unappetizing than to go into a house that smells of cabbage! The other reason is that I find after a fairly substantial first course, and with a pudding of some kind to follow, most people simply do not want a hot vegetable as well—a salad is quite enough, as well as being much lighter and more refreshing.

Obviously the menus are interchangeable as these things must be, but when you make alterations please remember the *balance* of the meal. This is most important. Without care you can end up with a meal like a Victorian wedding breakfast or send your guests home hungry. The intention surely is to give them a good, pleasant, adequate meal without their feeling like a snake that has swallowed a rabbit.

Please don't be frightened of attempting these meals. They are not in the least bit complicated, and I assure you that anybody who can read can cook.

All the menus will serve about six people unless otherwise stated. It is difficult to be specific about quantities as so much depends on individual capacity. I have given quite precise measurements, but if you are not a measurer and are used to cooking more or less 'by ear', please continue to do so; a spoonful either way will make very little difference to the finished dish—after all, you are cooking a dinner, not making an atomic bomb!

GEORGINA INFIELD

SPECIAL

OCCASIONS

MENU 1 *Buffet for Twenty*

Iced Salmon Mousse with Cucumber

Chili con Carne

Cheese Board and Celery

Mocha

Iced Salmon Mousse	2 large tins of salmon	$\frac{1}{2}$ pt single cream
	2 oz butter	2 lemons
	3 tablespoons flour	4 tablespoons gelatine
	1 pt milk	1 cucumber

Squeeze the lemons and add the gelatine. Set the bowl over hot water and heat until dissolved. Cool.

Purée or sieve the salmon until smooth.

Make a white sauce with the butter, flour, and milk (recipe on page 139). Add the sauce to the salmon. Taste and adjust seasoning. Add the cream and the gelatine mixture. Blend well together. Pour into either one very large or two smaller moulds. Refrigerate until set. Turn out on to one large or two small dishes and surround with thinly sliced cucumber.

Chili con Carne	5 lb minced beef	Large tin tomato juice
	2 lb brown dried kidney beans	Bay leaves
	2 large tins tomatoes	Salt, pepper
	2 lb onions	Chili powder
	6 tablespoons oil	

Soak the beans in water to cover overnight, then drain and cook gently in fresh water until tender.

Heat the oil gently in a large saucepan and add the onions, finely

2

sliced. Cook slowly until the onions are clear. Add the minced beef and fry, stirring constantly, until no trace of red remains in the meat. Add the salt, pepper, bay leaves, and chili powder. (The quantity of chili powder you add depends on how hot and spicy you like it. For this quantity of meat I usually add about 8 tablespoons, but if this seems too much to you add less and adjust it later.) Add the tomatoes and tomato juice, bring to the boil and simmer, stirring often, until the mixture is thick. Taste for seasoning, and add the brown kidney beans. Mix all well together and serve in bowls with spoons.

This can be made beforehand and reheated when required. It is perfect buffet food as it is easy to serve and to eat and there is nothing to cut. It is also a complete meal in itself and needs nothing but baskets of French bread served with it.

Cheese Board and Celery Arrange at least four kinds of cheese on a large, well-scrubbed board. A good mixture is Boursin garlic cheese, Camembert, Gruyère, and Gorgonzola. Have a couple of jars of well-scrubbed celery and a basket of crisp bread and cream crackers or water biscuits; lots of good unsalted butter goes without saying.

This is always terrifically popular, especially with the men, and you can continue to drink the same red wine that you served (I hope) with the Chili con Carne. Spanish red wine is splendid for a party and very reasonable.

Mocha   Serve this in long glasses with straws. I always get my party glasses from Woolworths.

4 pt strong, fresh coffee	1 lb plain chocolate
4 pt coffee ice cream	1 pt single cream

Break the chocolate into pieces put into a bowl. Cover with some of the coffee and heat over hot water until the chocolate is melted and smooth, stirring constantly. Blend all the ingredients together in a large bowl and beat until smooth. Serve very cold.

Shopping List

5 lb minced beef	1 lb plain chocolate
2 lemons	$\frac{1}{2}$ lb fresh ground coffee
1 cucumber	2 lb brown dried kidney beans
2 lb onions	Chili powder
3 heads of celery	Cheeses
2 large tins of salmon	4 pt coffee ice cream
Gelatine	1 pt milk
2 large tins tomatoes	$1\frac{1}{2}$ pt single cream
1 large tin tomato juice	French bread

MENU 2 *Celebration Dinner for Eight*

Consommé

Vol-au-vent Fruits du Mer

Roast Turkey and Chestnut Stuffing

Purée Potatoes

Chicory and Beetroot Salad

Iced Zabaglione

Consommé

1 marrow bone (split in two)	1 carrot
1 lb minced beef	1 stalk celery
2 onions	Salt and peppercorns

Put the marrow bones into a large saucepan and cover with 5 pints of cold water. Bring to the boil taking off the scum as it rises. When the surface is clear add the two onions *unpeeled* (this gives a good colour), the carrot, celery, a little salt, and some black peppercorns. Turn down the heat and simmer gently for 3 hours.

Crumble up the minced beef and add to the pot. Cook for another hour.

Strain through a sieve lined with a piece of linen. Allow to become cold (overnight if possible). Take off every scrap of fat. If you have cooked it slowly enough it should be quite clear. Reheat gently when required.

Vol-au-vent
Fruits du Mer

8 large vol-au-vent cases (these can be bought from any good pâtisserie)	$\frac{1}{2}$ pt single cream
	6 scallops
	$\frac{1}{2}$ lb peeled shrimps
2 oz butter	$\frac{1}{2}$ lb peeled scampi
2 tablespoons flour	1 tablespoon tomato purée
$\frac{1}{2}$ pt milk	Salt and pepper

Wash the scallops and cut them into quarters. Put into a saucepan and cover with the milk. Bring to the boil and simmer gently for 10 minutes. Drain them, reserving the milk. Melt the butter and stir in the flour. Cook for a few minutes stirring constantly then add the milk gradually. Simmer for 10 minutes then strain the sauce into a clean saucepan. Blend the cream and tomato purée together and add to the sauce. Season to taste with salt and pepper and add the shrimps, scampi, and scallops. Warm the vol-au-vent cases through in a low oven when required. Heat the filling at the same time and fill the cases with the mixture just before serving.

As you can see this can be made well ahead of time and left in the fridge until needed.

Roast Turkey and Chestnut Stuffing	1 12-lb turkey 4 oz butter 2 eating apples 2 onions	Bunch of parsley 1 tin chestnut purée Salt and pepper

STUFFING

Peel, core, and slice the apples. Melt 2 oz butter in a saucepan, add the apples and enough water just to cover them. Cook very slowly until the apples have melted to a purée. Stir in the chestnut purée, the onion and parsley (both minced finely). Add salt and pepper and cool the mixture.

Stuff the turkey fairly loosely and put into a baking tin. Season with salt and pepper and spread the breast of the bird with the remaining 2 oz of butter. Roast at 300° F. or Reg. 3 for 3 hours, basting every half-hour. Drain on to a serving dish and set in a warm place for half an hour before carving.

Purée Potatoes

3 lb potatoes	$\frac{1}{4}$ pt milk
2 oz butter	1 egg
Salt and pepper	

Peel and halve the potatoes; cook gently in salted water until they are very tender. Strain and mash very thoroughly, being careful to eliminate all the lumps. Beat in the butter, milk, egg, and pepper. Beat very well until light and creamy. (Where this recipe occurs elsewhere in the book, the quantity of potatoes should be about 2 lb for only 6 people.)

Chicory and Beetroot Salad

| 1 lb chicory | Sweet French dressing (recipe on p. 137) |
| 1 lb cooked beetroot | Chopped parsley |

Wipe the chicory with a clean cloth and cut into chunks with a stainless steel knife. Cube the peeled beetroot. Mix the two together in a glass bowl and sprinkle with chopped parsley. Pour the dressing over and mix well at the moment of service. This salad can be made early in the day and left to stand in the fridge or larder as long as it is not dressed.

Iced Zabaglione

| 10 egg yolks | 8 tablespoons Marsala |
| 8 tablespoons caster sugar | |

This is terribly simple if you have an electric mixer. Put all ingredients in a large bowl and set the bowl over a saucepan of hot water. Whisk steadily until the mixture rises right up the sides of the bowl in a golden foam. Remove the bowl from the hot water and continue whisking until the mixture is stone cold.

Set in the fridge for half an hour, then whisk for a further

10 minutes. Spoon into individual glasses and put in the fridge. Serve within 4 hours. In other words, make it in the afternoon and serve it in the evening.

This menu would obviously make a delicious Christmas dinner. Add Christmas pudding if you must.

Shopping List

1 12-lb turkey
1 lb minced beef
1 marrow bone
6 scallops
$\frac{1}{2}$ lb peeled shrimps
$\frac{1}{2}$ lb peeled scampi
4 onions
1 carrot
Celery
$\frac{1}{2}$ lb eating apples

3 lb potatoes
1 lb beetroot
1 lb chicory
Parsley
8 large vol-au-vent cases
1 small tin Italian tomato purée
1 tin chestnut purée
12 eggs
$\frac{1}{2}$ pt single cream
$\frac{1}{2}$ bottle Marsala

SUMMER
DINNERS

MENU 3 *Summer Dinner*

Charentais Melons with Port

Risotto al Pollo

Lettuce and Cucumber Salad

Lemon Ice Cream

Charentais
Melons with
Port

3 or 6 Charentais Melons according to size (and bank balance!)

6 teaspoons caster sugar
6 teaspoons Port (not vintage!)

If you are using 3 melons cut them in halves; if using 6 cut off the tops to form lids. Scoop out the seeds, being careful not to lose any of the juice. Sprinkle each portion with 1 teaspoon of sugar and 1 teaspoon of Port. Set in a cool place, preferably not the refrigerator, for 1 hour.

Risotto al
Pollo

1 boiling chicken (about 5 to 6 lb)
2 onions
12 oz Italian rice
½ pt milk
3 oz butter

3 oz grated Parmesan cheese
2 level tablespoons flour
Salt, black peppercorns
Bay leaves
Nutmeg
¼ pt single cream

Put the chicken into a deep saucepan, cover with cold water, bring to the boil, and skim the scum off as it rises. Add 1 onion, 3 bay leaves, salt and 6 whole black peppercorns. Turn down the heat and simmer very slowly until the chicken is tender. Melt 2 oz butter in a large sauté pan, add the other onion, finely chopped, and fry gently until the onion is transparent. Add the rice and fry gently, stirring constantly, for 2 minutes. Add enough of the chicken stock to cover the rice. Cook gently, stirring occasionally, until the stock is absorbed and the rice is tender. You will probably need more

10

stock but the rice should not be too liquid—the final consistency should be creamy. Spread the rice evenly in a large fireproof gratin dish.

Take the meat off the chicken. Remove the skin and cut the flesh into neat fillets. Lay the chicken on top of the rice. It should cover the rice completely in a single layer. Cover the chicken and rice with the sauce and heat through gently in a moderate oven, 335° F. or Reg. 3, for about 40 minutes, until the dish is hot through and lightly browned on top.

SAUCE

Melt the remaining butter in a saucepan and add the flour. Mix well and cook, stirring constantly, for 2 to 3 minutes. Add the milk and blend well. Add enough chicken stock, a little at a time, to make a smooth, creamy (but not too thick) sauce. Season the sauce with salt, pepper, and a generous scrape of nutmeg. Add the Parmesan cheese and the cream. Stir over a low heat until the cheese has melted. (This all sounds a bit of a performance but in fact it takes considerably longer to describe than to cook.)

This is a delicious dish, rich without being heavy, and it can be completely prepared the day before and kept in the fridge in its fireproof dish ready to be heated in the oven for the 40 minutes. It will come to no harm; in fact, if anything, it improves with keeping.

Lettuce and	1 lettuce	1 cucumber
Cucumber	French dressing (recipe on page 137)	
Salad		

Wash and dry the lettuce. Put round the outside of the bowl. Peel and finely slice the cucumber and put in the middle of the bowl. Pour the dressing over at the last moment.

Lemon	1 pt double cream	$\frac{1}{4}$ pt water
Ice Cream	4 egg yolks	$\frac{1}{4}$ pt fresh lemon juice
	6 oz sugar	

Dissolve the sugar in the water. Add the lemon juice, bring to the boil, and cook until reduced by half. Whip the egg yolks, add the

11

syrup slowly, and whip until cold. Whisk the cream until just stiff but do not overbeat. Fold the cream into the egg yolk mixture. Blend well. Freeze until just set but it should not be too hard. This can also be made the day before and left in the freezing compartment of the refrigerator until needed.

Shopping List

1 boiling chicken
3 or 6 Charentais melons
$\frac{1}{2}$ lb onions
1 lettuce
1 cucumber
3 lemons

1 lb Italian rice
Parmesan cheese
$\frac{1}{4}$ pt single cream
1 pt double cream
1 miniature bottle Port

Artichokes Vinaigrette

Mild Chicken Curry

Boiled Rice

Strawberry Delight

Artichokes   6 globe artichokes   French dressing (recipe on page 137)
Vinaigrette   Vinegar

Cut the stalks and the last two or three outside leaves off the artichokes so that they will stand evenly. Put them into a bowl of heavily salted cold water and leave to stand for an hour. Rinse them well under a running cold tap. Bring a very large saucepan of salted water to the boil. Add 3 tablespoons vinegar. Put in the artichokes, cover, turn down the heat and cook gently but steadily until they are tender. This should take about 20 minutes. Test one by digging a small sharp knife into the base of the artichoke. It should feel tender and the knife should go in easily.

Put the artichokes upside down on to a grid and leave until all the liquid has drained out of them and they are quite cold. Push the leaves open slightly so that they look like a flower. Arrange on a large flat dish and serve a sauceboat full of French dressing separately. Supply a couple of empty plates to put the debris on, finger bowls, and a knife and fork for eating the heart (which is the best part).

Mild   1 4-lb boiled chicken   3 tablespoons curry powder
Chicken   2 carrots   2 pt stock
Curry   2 onions   2 oz butter
    2 eating apples $\frac{1}{4}$ pt single cream
    2 bananas   2 teaspoons arrowroot
    4 tablespoons sultanas

Take all the flesh off the boiled chicken and cut into cubes. Peel and chop the carrots and onions. Melt the butter and cook the carrots and onions until they soften. Add the curry powder and the peeled chopped apples. Cook gently for 5 minutes. Add the chopped bananas and 1 pint stock (if you have no home-made stock, use bouillon cubes). Cook gently for 15 minutes, then add the chicken and the sultanas. Dissolve the arrowroot in the remaining stock, add, and heat through. Add the cream, bring to the boil, and serve. This can be made in advance up to the point where you add the cream, but you must heat it right through before you add the cream.

Serve with mango chutney.

| *Boiled Rice* | 12 oz Italian rice | Salt |
| | 2 tablespoons oil | |

Bring a large saucepan of water to the boil. Add salt and oil. Throw in rice. Cook steadily for 12 minutes. Strain the rice through a metal colander. Rinse with cold water to get rid of the starch. Set the colander over a saucepan of water and cover it with the lid of the saucepan. Put the whole contraption over a gentle heat and steam the rice until hot through and dry and fluffy. The rice will keep hot for a long time this way and will never go soggy. Although patna rice is traditional with curry I use Italian rice for everything—it is much less inclined to coagulate and has a better flavour.

14

Strawberry	¾ lb frozen strawberries in sugar	1 oz gelatine
Delight	1 pt single cream	3 tablespoons Cointreau

Purée ½ lb strawberries and mix with the cream. Melt the gelatine with the Cointreau over hot water, cool, add to the strawberries and cream. Whip like mad until fluffy. Pour into a serving dish and refrigerate. Garnish with the remaining ¼ lb strawberries. This can be made in advance.

Shopping List

1 4-lb boiling chicken
6 globe artichokes
½ lb carrots
½ lb onions
½ lb eating apples
2 bananas
¾ lb frozen strawberries in sugar

Sultanas
Gelatine
Bouillon cubes
1 lb Italian rice
Mango chutney
1¼ pt single cream
1 miniature bottle of Cointreau

MENU 5 *Summer Dinner*

Ratatouille en Salade

Escalope de Veau Viennoise

Sauté Potatoes

French Beans

Raspberries and Redcurrants

Ratatouille
en Salade

2 Spanish onions
2 aubergines
2 green peppers
½ lb courgettes

1 medium tin tomatoes
3 cloves garlic
Salt, pepper, oil

Cover a fireproof casserole with oil to the depth of ¼ inch. Peel 2 Spanish onions and slice thinly. Peel and chop the garlic. Put the onions and garlic into the pan and cook gently until soft and yellow. Take the core and seeds out of the peppers, cut into squares, and add to the pot. Wash the aubergines and the courgettes, slice the ends off but do not peel, and cut into chunks. Add to the pot with salt and pepper and the tin of tomatoes. Mix well, put into a fairly low oven, 300° F. or Reg. 2, uncovered. Cook slowly until all the vegetables are very soft but not mushy. Allow to become absolutely cold. This can be made the day before.

Serve with hot French bread.

Escalope
de Veau
Viennoise

6 veal escalopes
2 eggs
Soft white breadcrumbs

2 tablespoons oil
3 oz butter
2 lemons

Beat the eggs. Dip the escalopes into the egg and then the breadcrumbs. Make sure they are well coated. Warm the oil in a frying pan. Add the butter and heat until the butter foams. Fry the

16

escalopes until they are golden brown. Drain well. Arrange on a fireproof dish. Heat gently through when required and garnish with quarters of lemon. Served this way, escalopes can be cooked ahead of time quite satisfactorily.

Sauté Potatoes 2 lb potatoes Oil

Boil the potatoes in their skins until just tender. Peel and cut into squares. Heat oil in a chip pan. Deep fry the potatoes fairly slowly until brown and crisp. Classically these should be cooked in shallow fat, but I have found them more satisfactory cooked in this way; they are crisper and less greasy.

French Beans $1\frac{1}{2}$ lb French beans 1 oz butter

Top and tail the French beans. Cook gently in salted water until just tender. Drain and toss in melted butter until very hot.

Raspberries $1\frac{1}{2}$ lb raspberries 4 oz sugar
and 1 lb redcurrants
Redcurrants

Pick over the raspberries but do not wash. Take the redcurrants off their stalks and rinse briefly in cold water. Drain thoroughly. Mix the fruits together with the sugar. Leave in a cold place or the refrigerator for at least 2 hours.
Serve with thick cream.

Shopping List

6 veal escalopes
2 Spanish onions
2 aubergines
2 green peppers
$\frac{1}{2}$ lb courgettes
2 lemons
2 lb potatoes

$1\frac{1}{2}$ lb French beans
$1\frac{1}{2}$ lb raspberries
1 lb redcurrants
1 medium tin tomatoes
$\frac{1}{2}$ pt cream
French bread

17

MENU 6 *Summer Dinner*

Asparagus

Salmon

New Potatoes

Peas

Cucumber Salad ·

Strawberries Romanoff

This is known in our family as the economy menu. When we are really broke we have this to cheer ourselves up. Then we are even more hard up trying to pay for it!

Asparagus The great thing about asparagus is to have lots of it. It's better to have none at all than not enough.

3 lb asparagus	Butter

Wash and clean the asparagus and cut off the hard ends. Tie into 6 bunches. Bring a large saucepan of salted water to the boil. Put in the asparagus and simmer gently until just tender. This should take about 20 minutes but it varies with the age and thickness of the asparagus. Lift the bunches out and drain well.

Lay in a metal colander and reheat over a saucepan of boiling water when required. Serve with a large sauceboat of melted butter; at least $\frac{1}{2}$ lb will be needed.

Salmon

6 salmon steaks
1½ lemons
1 onion
1 bay leaf

Salt
Black peppercorns
Watercress

Lay the salmon steaks in one layer in a shallow pan (a roasting tin does very well). Cut ½ lemon and the onion into thin slices and strew them over the salmon, together with the bay leaf, salt, and half a dozen black peppercorns. Cover with cold water. Bring slowly to a simmer, and cook on the lowest possible heat for exactly 7 minutes. Drain well and serve garnished with lemon quarters and watercress on a hot dish.

New Potatoes

2 lb new potatoes
½ oz butter

1 tablespoon chopped parsley

Scrape the potatoes and cook in salted water until just tender. Drain well, put back in the saucepan with the butter and parsley, and toss over a low heat until very hot and well coated with parsley.

Peas

3 lb peas
1 lettuce
2 oz butter

6 cubes sugar
Salt

Shell the peas. Wash the lettuce and cut into ribbons. Put the peas, lettuce, butter, sugar, and salt all together in a saucepan. Cover closely and cook extremely slowly until the peas are very tender. This takes quite a long time. Reheat gently when required.

Cucumber Salad

1 cucumber
1 tablespoon vinegar

2 teaspoons caster sugar
Salt

Peel the cucumber and cut into wafer-thin slices. Lay on a flat dish. Mix together the vinegar, sugar, and salt and sprinkle the dressing over the cucumber. Leave to stand 1 to 2 hours.

19

| *Strawberries* | 2½ lb fresh strawberries | 6 tablespoons caster sugar |
| *Romanoff* | ½ pt double cream | 3 tablespoons Cointreau |

Wash the strawberries, hull them, and put 2 lb into a serving bowl. Crush the remaining ½ lb very fine. Add the sugar and Cointreau and stir until the sugar is dissolved. Add the cream and blend well. Pour the sauce over the strawberries. Leave in the refrigerator 1 hour.

Shopping List

6 salmon steaks
3 lb asparagus
2 lemons
½ lb onions
1 bunch watercress
2 lb new potatoes
1 bunch parsley

3 lb peas
1 lettuce
1 cucumber
2½ lb strawberries
1 lb butter
½ pt double cream
1 miniature bottle Cointreau

MENU 7 *Summer Dinner*

Chicken Liver Pâté

Crab Soufflé

Lettuce and Cucumber Salad

Raspberry Mille Feuilles

This is a fairly light meal, good for a hot day or on a Sunday evening when your guests may have had a big lunch.

Chicken Liver Pâté

1 lb chicken livers
6 oz butter
1 onion

2 tablespoons Brandy
Salt and pepper

Chop and cook the onion in 2 oz butter until it is very soft (but not browned). Add the chicken livers, cover and cook, stirring occasionally until they are very tender. Put the whole lot through a blender (if you haven't got one you will have to use a sieve but of course it makes more work). Put in a bowl and add the remaining 4 oz butter (softened), the Brandy and seasoning. Mix very thoroughly until well blended. Press down into a china pot and smooth the top evenly. Put in the refrigerator for at least 24 hours.

Serve with plenty of thinly sliced, hot toast.

Crab Soufflé

1 lb white crab meat (fresh, frozen, or tinned)
6 egg yolks
8 egg whites

2 oz butter
3 tablespoons flour
½ to ¾ pt milk
Salt and pepper

Make a fairly thick béchamel sauce (recipe on page 139) with the butter, flour, milk, salt, and pepper. Cool slightly, add the egg yolks, and mix well. Stir in the flaked crab and mix well again.

21

Whisk the egg whites until stiff but not dry and fold lightly into the crab mixture. Turn into either 2 large buttered soufflé dishes or 12 individual soufflé dishes. If you are using 2 large ones bake at 350° F. or Reg. 4 for 30 minutes. If you use individual dishes, bake at 350° F. or Reg. 4 for 20 minutes.

I never attempt to make one very large soufflé. By the time it is cooked in the centre it is dry on the outside.

Lettuce and Cucumber Salad

As for Menu 3, see page 11.

Raspberry Mille Feuilles

1 packet frozen puff pastry $\frac{1}{2}$ pt double cream
2 punnets raspberries   Caster sugar

Roll the pastry into a strip 4 inches wide and $\frac{1}{4}$ inch thick. Bake in a hot oven, 425° F. or Reg. 7, until well risen and brown. Cool. Cut carefully in half. Spread 1$\frac{1}{2}$ punnets of raspberries evenly on the bottom half. Sprinkle thickly with caster sugar. Whip the cream. Spread half of it over the raspberries. Cover with the pastry lid. With a very sharp knife cut into 6 even strips. Cover each strip with cream and garnish with the remaining raspberries. Serve very cold.

Shopping List

1 lb chicken livers   1 packet frozen puff pastry
1 lb white crab meat $\frac{1}{2}$ lb butter
1 onion   8 eggs
1 lettuce   1 pt milk
1 cucumber $\frac{1}{2}$ pt double cream
2 punnets raspberries   Brandy

MENU 8 *Summer Dinner*

Melon and Parma Ham

Salmon Trout and Cucumber

Potato Salad

Mayonnaise

Hot Caramelized Apple Soufflé

Melon and
Parma Ham

1 large Honeydew melon $\frac{1}{2}$ lb Parma ham (cut wafer thin)

Cut the melon into 12 narrow sections. Cut off the rind. Wrap each section in a slice of Parma ham. Serve on a large dish.

Salmon Trout
and Cucumber

1 3½-lb salmon trout (or 2   Oil
   smaller ones)   Tinfoil
Salt and pepper   1 cucumber

Wash the fish and season it. Brush a large sheet of tinfoil with oil. Lay the fish on it and seal up completely. Bake in a medium oven, 400° F. or Reg. 6, for 40 minutes (or if you are using two smaller fish bake for 25 minutes). Unwrap and allow to cool enough to handle. Take off the skin and the head. Lay on a large flat dish and allow to become completely cold. Peel the cucumber and slice thinly. Put a line of cucumber slices down the centre of the fish and surround the fish with the rest of the cucumber slices. Serve cold but do not cook too far ahead of time (2 to 3 hours is quite long enough).

Potato Salad

2 lb new potatoes   Salt and pepper
3 tablespoons chopped parsley   1 tablespoon wine vinegar
1 finely chopped onion   6 tablespoons oil

23

Scrape the potatoes and cook gently in salted water until just tender. Drain. Cut them in slices while they are still warm. Add the parsley, onion, seasoning, oil, and vinegar. Mix thoroughly but carefully, as they must not break. Allow to become cold but do not refrigerate if you can help it as this takes away the flavour.

MAYONNAISE
Home-made mayonnaise should be used for all purposes. There is a recipe on page 138.

Hot
Caramelized
Apple Soufflé

| 2 lb cooking apples | 6 eggs |
| 12 oz caster sugar | |

Melt 6 oz sugar with 6 tablespoons water and cook, without stirring, to a rich golden brown. Pour into a deep fireproof dish or soufflé mould and coat the inside thoroughly by tilting the mould in all directions. Peel, core, and slice the apples. Put into a saucepan with $\frac{1}{4}$ pt water and cook slowly, stirring occasionally until it is a smooth purée. Add the remaining 6 oz sugar and continue cooking slowly until very thick. Add the 6 egg yolks one by one, beating well after each addition. Whisk the egg whites until very stiff and fold into the apples. Pour this mixture into the caramelized mould and stand the dish in a tin with 2 inches of water in it and bake at 335° F. or Reg. 3, for $1\frac{1}{2}$ hours. Allow to stand for 5 minutes before turning out on to a dish. Take care when you turn it out. It breaks very easily but it is worth the trouble.

Shopping List

1 $3\frac{1}{2}$-lb salmon trout	2 lb cooking apples
1 large Honeydew melon	1 onion
1 cucumber	6 eggs
2 lb new potatoes	$\frac{1}{2}$ lb Parma ham
Parsley	

MENU 9   *Summer Dinner*

Eggs Mimosa

Sautéd Kidneys with Boiled Rice

Lettuce Salad

Coffee Soufflé

Eggs Mimosa   12 eggs   Watercress
$\frac{1}{2}$ pt home-made mayonnaise (recipe on page 138)

Hard boil the eggs and peel them. Slice 9 of them in half and lay them cut side down on a flat dish. Cover them with mayonnaise. Put the remaining 3 eggs through a sieve, holding the sieve over the egg mayonnaise so that the sieved egg falls lightly on to the mayonnaise creating a decorative pattern. Put sprigs of watercress round the edge of the dish and serve very cold.

Sautéd   2 lb ox kidneys   2 bay leaves
Kidneys 1 Spanish onion   1 teaspoon arrowroot
           2 oz butter or good dripping   Salt and pepper
           1 medium tin tomatoes

Cut the kidneys into thin slices, cutting out the core and any fat that may be adhering to them. Put in a deep bowl and pour a kettle of boiling water over them. Allow to stand until cold. Drain well in a colander and rinse under the cold tap. This preliminary blanching takes away any unpleasant taste that kidneys can sometimes have. Melt the butter in a fireproof casserole and throw in the chopped onion, and cook until pale gold. Add the drained kidneys and fry slowly, covered, for 10 minutes. Add the tomatoes, bay leaves, and seasoning. Put into the oven, uncovered, and cook at 300° F. or Reg. 2, for 1$\frac{1}{2}$ hours stirring occasionally. Half an hour before serving take out a cupful of the juices from the

25   S.N.—3

kidneys and blend with the arrowroot until quite smooth. Pour back over the kidneys, mix well, and replace in the oven for the last half-hour. This dish can be made ahead of time or even the day before and reheated without deterioration. Serve with boiled rice.

Boiled Rice   Cook as for Menu 4, see page 14.

Lettuce Salad   The same salad as for Menu 3 but without the cucumber and using 2 lettuces (see page 11).

Coffee Soufflé

1 oz gelatine	$\frac{1}{4}$ pt single cream
6 tablespoons strong black coffee	$\frac{1}{4}$ pt double cream
6 eggs	Walnuts
6 level tablespoons caster sugar	

Soften the gelatine in the black coffee and melt over hot water. Allow to cool. Separate the eggs. Whisk the egg whites until stiff; set aside. Whip the egg yolks and sugar together until thick and pale. Add the coffee and gelatine mixture and the single cream. Blend well. Fold in the egg whites, pour into a serving bowl, and refrigerate until set. Whisk the double cream until thick and put in mounds all round the edges of the soufflé. Decorate with walnut halves and sprinkle the centre with a little grated chocolate if you have any. Serve very cold.

Shopping List

2 lb ox kidneys	1 lb Italian rice
1 Spanish onion	Coffee
2 lettuces	Gelatine
Watercress	18 eggs
Walnuts	$\frac{1}{4}$ pt single cream
1 medium tin tomatoes	$\frac{1}{4}$ pt double cream

MENU 10 *Summer Dinner*

Avocado Vinaigrette

Veal Chops with Tarragon

Purée Potatoes

Salsify Provençal

Pêche Brûlée

Avocado   3 large avocado pears   4 tablespoons oil
Vinaigrette 1 tablespoon wine vinegar   Salt and pepper

Blend the salt, pepper, oil, and vinegar together. Cut the pears in halves. Take out the stones and fill the central cavities with the dressing, serve on individual plates with a teaspoon to eat them with. Do not cut them until you are ready to eat them, otherwise the cut edges will go black.

Veal Chops   6 large Dutch veal chops   Salt and pepper
with Tarragon 1 oz butter   1 tablespoon chopped
                                                  tarragon (dried or fresh)

Season the chops with salt and pepper. Melt the butter and fry the chops until lightly browned on both sides. Put the chops in a roasting tin. Pour over the juices from the frying pan and sprinkle the tarragon over the chops. Roast in a medium oven, 400° F. or Reg. 6, for half an hour, turning the chops over at half time. Serve on a hot dish with the skimmed juices poured over them.

Purée Potatoes   As for Menu 2, see page 7.

27

Salsify This is a delicious vegetable, sometimes called oyster plant. It is
Provençal quite easy to grow and you can buy it in Soho and, occasionally, at
Harrods.

3 lb salsify	1 oz butter
1 small tin tomatoes	1 tablespoon chopped parsley
1 onion	Salt and pepper
2 cloves garlic	Vinegar

Peel the salsify and cut into two-inch lengths. Drop the pieces into
a bowl of cold water spiked with a little vinegar. When you are
ready to cook the salsify, rinse the pieces under the cold tap, cover
with cold water, and bring to the boil. Salt lightly, turn down the
heat and simmer until just tender. Drain. Half an hour before you
are ready to eat, melt the butter in a sauté pan, throw in the onion
and garlic, both finely chopped, and cook slowly until soft. Add the
tomatoes and cook until thick. Add the drained salsify and chopped
parsley. Cook gently for a further 10 minutes. Serve very hot.

Pêche Brûlée   6 large ripe yellow-fleshed $\frac{1}{2}$ pt whipped cream
    peaches   6 tablespoons brown sugar

Peel and slice the peaches. Put into a fireproof dish. Cover with
whipped cream. Put in the coldest part of the refrigerator and
leave for at least 2 hours. Make the grill as hot as it is possible.
Sprinkle the brown sugar over the whipped cream in a thick layer.

28

Put the dish under the grill and allow the sugar to melt and caramelize (see Glossary, page 140), forming a hard crust over the top of the pudding, but take care that the sugar does not burn. Serve at once. This cannot wait a second, otherwise it will spoil.

This is a lovely pudding but it is only really successful with the big fleshy peaches that are obtainable in the late summer.

Shopping List   6 large Dutch veal chops (they must be Dutch, the English ones are the wrong shape and are too small)
3 avocado pears
2 lb potatoes
3 lb salsify

Parsley
6 large yellow peaches
1 onion
Tarragon (fresh or dried)
1 small tin tomatoes
Wine vinegar
$\frac{1}{2}$ pt double cream

MENU 11 *Summer Dinner*

Vichyssoise

Baby Chickens with Almonds

New Potatoes

Lettuce Salad

Orange Chiffon

Vichyssoise

1 lb leeks
1 lb potatoes
1 onion
2 oz butter

3 pt chicken stock
½ pt single cream
1 bunch chives
Salt and pepper

Clean and chop the potatoes and the onion, and the white part of the leeks. Melt the butter in a saucepan and throw in the vegetables. Cover and allow to cook very slowly for 5 minutes. Do not allow to brown. Cover with the stock (4 chicken bouillon cubes will do), bring to the boil, and cook slowly and steadily uncovered until the vegetables are very soft. Put the whole panful through a sieve or purée in a blender. Taste and season. Allow to become ice cold and stir in the cream. Serve very cold in individual cups with a teaspoon of finely chopped chives sprinkled on each portion at the moment of service.

Baby Chickens with Almonds

6 petits poussins (these little chickens should not weigh more than 1 lb each)

¼ lb flaked almonds
Butter
Salt and pepper

Spread the breasts of the poussins with a little soft butter. Sprinkle with salt and pepper. Roast in a fairly hot oven, 425° F. or Reg. 7, until brown and tender (about half an hour). Dish the chickens on

30

to a fireproof serving dish. Keep warm. Throw the almonds into the juices and cook over a fast heat until the almonds become light brown. Pour the whole panful over the chickens and serve. This will keep hot without deterioration for about 20 minutes, and so it can be dished up just before you sit down to your first course.

New Potatoes   As for Menu 6, see page 19.

Lettuce Salad   As for Menu 9, see pages 26 and 11.

Orange   4 oranges   4 tablespoons marmalade
Chiffon   4 eggs   1 oz gelatine
                  4 tablespoons sugar $\frac{1}{2}$ pt double cream

Take out 2 tablespoons of cream, whip it, and reserve it for decoration.

Grate the rind of the oranges and squeeze out the juice. Dissolve the gelatine in the orange juice in a bowl over hot water. Cool. Whisk the egg whites until stiff. Set aside. Melt the marmalade. Cool. Whip the egg yolks and sugar until thick and pale. Stir in the orange peel, orange juice and gelatine, and the marmalade. Mix well, stir in the cream and fold in the egg whites. Pour into a serving bowl and refrigerate.

Just before serving decorate with the whipped cream and glacé cherries or grated chocolate.

Shopping List   6 petits poussins   2 lettuces
                  1 lb leeks   4 oranges
                  1 onion $\frac{1}{4}$ lb flaked almonds
                  1 lb potatoes   4 bouillon cubes
                  Chives   Gelatine
                  2 lb new potatoes $\frac{1}{2}$ pt double cream
                  Parsley $\frac{1}{2}$ pt single cream

MENU 12 *Summer Dinner*

Tarama Salata

Ham in Cream Sauce

New Potatoes

Tomato and Pepper Salad

Jellied Apples

Tarama	1 lb smoked cods' roe	1 lemon (squeezed)
Salata	2 teacups soft white breadcrumbs	1 tablespoon chopped parsley
	1 tablespoon minced onion	8 tablespoons oil
		Pepper

Mix the roe in a bowl with the onion and lemon juice. Add the oil gradually, stirring all the time until it is smooth. Pepper lightly then stir in the breadcrumbs. Blend well together. Pile into a bowl and sprinkle with chopped parsley. Serve very cold with hot toast.

Ham in	$1\frac{1}{4}$ lb sliced cooked ham	$\frac{1}{2}$ pt white wine or Vermouth
Cream Sauce	1 chopped onion	$\frac{1}{2}$ pt single cream
	2 teaspoons tomato purée	2 oz butter
	1 pt stock	

SAUCE
Melt the butter. Cook the chopped onion slowly in the butter until it is soft. Add the tomato purée, stock, and wine. Bring to the boil, turn down the heat, and simmer gently for 1 hour. Strain this mixture into a large shallow pan. Add the cream and heat gently.

Put the slices of ham into the sauce and simmer, very slowly, until the ham is hot through. Serve very hot. The sauce can be made well ahead of time and just heated through with the ham at the last minute. To heat the ham takes less than 5 minutes.

32

New Potatoes   As for Menu 6, see page 19.

Tomato and   1 lb tomatoes   French dressing (recipe on
Pepper Salad   2 green peppers   page 137)

Slice the tomatoes and arrange in circles on a flat dish. Wash the peppers and cut out the core and the seeds. Cut into rounds. Arrange the pepper slices over the tomatoes and sprinkle with French dressing. Leave for one hour in a cold place.

Jellied Apples   ½ pt water   1 tablespoon grated lemon peel
                     8 oz sugar   2 tablespoons grated orange peel
                     4 drops cochineal   1 teaspoon cinnamon
                     6 medium cooking apples

Put water, sugar, cochineal, lemon peel, orange peel, and cinnamon together in a wide shallow pan. Bring to the boil and stir until the sugar is dissolved. Peel the apples but leave whole. Turn the heat down as low as it will go. Put in the apples and cook, uncovered, for 1½ hours, turning the apples over every half-hour. This must not boil otherwise the fruit will disintegrate. Lay the apples on a dish and pour over the syrup. When it is cold it should set to a light jelly. The whole apples, scarlet coloured, in the clear red jelly flecked with orange and lemon peel, is most attractive and unusual.

Shopping List   1¼ lb sliced ham   2 green peppers
                    Parsley   6 cooking apples
                    1 lemon   1 lb smoked cods' roe
                    1 orange   1 tube Italian tomato purée
                    ½ lb onions   1 bouillon cube
                    2 lb new potatoes   ½ pt single cream
                    1 lb tomatoes   ½ pt white wine or Vermouth

MENU 13 *Summer Dinner*

Iced Watercress and Potato Soup

Chicken Croquettes

Leaf Spinach

Banana Meringue

Iced	2 bunches watercress	$\frac{1}{2}$ pt milk
Watercress	1 lb potatoes (peeled weight)	$\frac{1}{2}$ pt single cream
and Potato	1 oz butter	Salt and pepper
Soup	2 pt chicken stock	

Wash the watercress thoroughly under the cold tap. Take out the six best sprigs and reserve them. Drain the rest and chop coarsely. Melt the butter in a saucepan, add the watercress and the potatoes (peeled and sliced). Cover and stew gently in the butter for 10 minutes. Pour over the stock (which can be made from 3 chicken bouillon cubes), bring to the boil, and cook steadily until the potatoes are very soft. Put the panful through a sieve, taste, and season with salt and pepper. Add the milk and cream. Serve ice cold in individual cups with a sprig of watercress on each cup.

Chicken	1 lb cooked chicken	$\frac{1}{2}$ pt milk
Croquettes	$\frac{3}{4}$ lb chicken livers	2 eggs
	4 oz pâté de foie	Breadcrumbs
	3 oz butter	Salt and pepper
	2 tablespoons flour	Cooking oil

Cook the chicken livers in 1 oz butter. Cool. Mince the chicken and chicken livers together. Put into a bowl and add the pâté. Mix well.

Make a béchamel sauce (recipe on page 139) with the remaining butter, the flour and milk (you may need a little more milk; the sauce should be very thick but not stodgy). Mix the white sauce with the chicken mixture. Blend well. Allow to become absolutely cold. It is easier to handle if you can leave it in the fridge overnight. Roll the mixture into balls and shape into croquettes (either small round patties or cork shapes). Dip into beaten egg and breadcrumbs twice to make a good coating. Refrigerate again. Just before you are ready to eat heat a large pan of oil and deep fry the croquettes until they are crisp and brown. They can be kept warm for about 15 minutes but no longer.

Leaf Spinach	5 lb spinach	Salt and pepper
	4 oz butter	

Wash the spinach very thoroughly in several lots of water and under a running tap, and pull the leaves off the centre spines. Press into a large saucepan, cover and cook gently for 10 minutes. The spinach will shrink and give off its water. Drain in a colander pressing down to expel all the moisture. Put into a clean saucepan with the butter and seasoning. Cook gently stirring constantly until tender. This can be reheated gently without harm. Personally I always use frozen leaf spinach. If you follow my example you will want two 1-lb packets. It seems to me to be the only vegetable that does not deteriorate and lose flavour with the freezing process.

Banana	8 ripe bananas	3 egg whites
Meringue	$\frac{1}{2}$ pt whipped cream	4 tablespoons caster sugar
	2 teaspoons instant coffee	

Mash the bananas to a smooth purée. It must be absolutely free from lumps. Add the coffee and fold in the whipped cream. Blend well and put into a fireproof serving dish. Whisk the egg whites until stiff, add the sugar and whisk again until shiny. Pile on top of the banana mixture. Spread well so that there are no gaps between meringue and the dish. Put into a cool oven 200° F. or

Reg. 2, until the meringue is pale biscuit colour and crisp on top. All should be left to become very cold.

This must be eaten on the same day that it is made.

Shopping List

1 small chicken
¾ lb chicken livers
2 bunches watercress
1½ lb potatoes
8 ripe bananas
5 lb spinach or 2 1-lb packets
    frozen spinach

3 bouillon cubes
4 oz pâté de foie
½ pt double cream
½ pt single cream
1 pt milk

Pea Soup

Steak Tartare

Lettuce Salad

Vanilla Soufflé with Strawberries

Pea Soup

1 lb frozen peas	2½ pt water
1 ham-bone	¼ pt single cream
1 oz butter	Salt and pepper
2 tablespoons chopped mint	

Bring the water to the boil, add the ham-bone, and simmer for half an hour. Add the peas and mint and simmer 15 minutes. Take out the ham-bone and put the saucepanful through a sieve or purée in a blender. Put into a clean saucepan and season. Add the butter and cream and reheat gently. Do not allow it to boil but serve very hot.

Steak Tartare You either will like this very much indeed or find it absolutely revolting. If you like it, check with your guests first to make sure they will eat it, as some people find the idea of raw meat repellent.

2½ lb best quality rump or fillet steak	6 egg yolks
1 finely chopped onion	4 tablespoons oil
3 tablespoons chopped parsley	1 tablespoon vinegar
2 tablespoons chopped capers	2 teaspoons Worcester sauce
3 gherkins finely chopped	Salt, Black pepper

Cut every scrap of fat and gristle off the meat. Put through a mincer. Add the onion, parsley, capers, and gherkins. Mix well.

37

Add the egg yolks, oil, vinegar, seasoning, and Worcester sauce. Blend very well again. Divide into 6 even portions and shape into round patties. Serve very cold.

A side plate of hot French fried potatoes is delicious with this, although rather unorthodox.

Lettuce Salad   As for Menu 9, see pages 26 and 11.

Vanilla   4 eggs $\frac{1}{4}$ pt water
Soufflé with   6 tablespoons vanilla sugar $\frac{3}{4}$ pt whipped cream
Strawberries   (recipe on page 139)   1 lb strawberries
$\frac{1}{2}$ oz gelatine

Melt the gelatine in $\frac{1}{4}$ pt water in a bowl over hot water. Cool. Separate the eggs. Whisk the egg whites until stiff—set aside.

Whip the egg yolks and sugar in a bowl over hot water until thick. Add the gelatine and $\frac{1}{2}$ pt whipped cream. Fold in the egg whites. Pour the mixture into a ring mould and refrigerate until set. Turn out on to a flat dish. Fill the centre with $\frac{3}{4}$ lb strawberries, and decorate with the remaining cream and strawberries.

Shopping List	2$\frac{1}{2}$ lb steak (rump or fillet)	1 lb frozen peas
	1 ham-bone	Capers
	Mint	3 gherkins
	Parsley	Gelatine
	2 lettuces	10 eggs
	1 lb strawberries	$\frac{1}{4}$ pt single cream
	1 onion	$\frac{3}{4}$ pt double cream

Piperade

Cold Roast Beef

Russian Salad

Summer Pudding

Piperade

1 Spanish onion
2 green peppers
1 medium tin tomatoes
8 eggs

Salt and pepper
6 tablespoons oil
3 slices bread

Heat 3 tablespoons oil in a saucepan. Add the finely chopped onion and cook gently until soft. Add the deseeded, sliced green peppers and cook gently until the peppers are soft. Add the tomatoes and cook gently until thick. Beat the eggs well and pour into the vegetables. Cook gently, stirring all the time until the eggs are scrambled but still creamy. Pile on to a hot dish and serve at once surrounded by the bread which has been cut into quarters and fried until golden in the remaining 3 tablespoons oil.

Cold Roast Beef

3 lb rolled sirloin

Salt and pepper

Take a piece of boned, rolled sirloin and season. Roast at 425° F. or Reg. 7 for an hour basting at 10-minute intervals with its own fat. Drain and allow to become completely cold. Cut into fine slices and arrange on a large flat dish.

Russian Salad

$\frac{1}{2}$ lb carrots
$\frac{1}{2}$ lb potatoes
$\frac{1}{2}$ lb beetroot
1 tin tunny fish
1 tin petits pois

2 large sweet and sour pickled cucumbers
$\frac{1}{2}$ pt home-made mayonnaise (recipe on page 138)

Cook the peeled carrots and potatoes gently until just tender. Drain, cool, and cut into fine dice. Peel the cooked beetroot and cut into small dice. Drain the petits pois. Mix the potatoes, carrots, beetroot, and petits pois together gently. Chop the cucumbers very finely and add to the vegetables. Drain the tunny fish, shred very small, and stir into the mayonnaise. Mix the tunny fish, mayonnaise, and the vegetables together gently but thoroughly. Pile into a mound in a serving dish and serve very cold.

| Summer Pudding | 1½ lb raspberries | 6 oz sugar |
| | ½ lb redcurrants | Sliced white bread |

Line completely a deep china dish (a soufflé dish does very well) with slices of dry bread with the crusts cut off. The dish must be completely lined without a gap anywhere. Take the redcurrants off their stalks. Put the redcurrants and sugar in a saucepan. Heat gently, stirring constantly, until the sugar is dissolved and the juice starts to run from the redcurrants. Add the raspberries and cook exactly 3 minutes. Drain the fruits, reserving the juice, and fill the bread-lined mould with the fruit. Cover completely with more slices of bread. Put a plate on top which just fits inside the dish, weight the plate lightly and put in the refrigerator for 24 hours.

Turn out the next day and serve with the reserved juice as a sauce. You can mix the juice with an equal volume of thick cream, which is even more delicious.

Shopping List	3 lb rolled sirloin of beef	1 medium tin tomatoes
	1 Spanish onion	1 tin tunny fish
	2 green peppers	1 tin petits pois
	½ lb carrots	2 large sweet and sour
	½ lb potatoes	pickled cucumbers
	½ lb beetroot	8 eggs
	1½ lb raspberries	1 sliced white loaf
	½ lb redcurrants	

WINTER
DINNERS

MENU 16 *Winter Dinner*

Minestrone Soup

Assiette Anglaise

Chicory and Beetroot Salad, Jacket Potatoes

Apple Charlotte

Minestrone Soup

1 large Spanish onion
2 cloves of garlic
1 lb carrots
1 lb leeks
½ lb pasta (spaghetti broken into short lengths, or other shapes such as bows, shells, or letters)
3 pt stock (bouillon cubes will do)

Grated Parmesan cheese
3 tablespoons oil
1 small tin of tomatoes
½ lb dried red beans (you can get these in any good delicatessen)
Salt and pepper

First soak the beans overnight in water to cover. Then simmer in lightly salted water until just tender, drain and set aside.

Peel and chop all the vegetables. There is no need to be too neat as this is after all a peasant dish, but the pieces must be fairly small.

Put the oil into a large saucepan and heat gently. Add the onion and garlic. Cover and simmer slowly for 5 minutes. Add the carrots, leeks, and red beans. Cover and simmer again for a further 5 minutes. Then give the vegetables a good stir and add the tomatoes and the stock. Simmer at the same slow speed, but uncovered this time, for half an hour. Then add the pasta and salt and pepper and simmer a further 15 minutes, stirring occasionally. Serve with a bowl of grated Parmesan cheese.

Assiette Anglaise

½ lb ham (on the bone if you can get it)
½ lb tongue (tinned is much better than fresh)
¼ lb salami (Italian only please, nothing else will do)

¼ lb kassler (smoked pork loin, very good)
¾ lb sliced liver sausage (smoked is good)
Parsley or watercress

42

Get the largest dish you can find, as this looks awful crammed together on too small a dish. Lay the meats out in neat symmetrical lines and put a bouquet of parsley or watercress in the centre.

Chicory and   As for Menu 2, see page 7.
Beetroot Salad

Jacket   Scrub well a large potato (weighing approximately ½ lb) for each
Potatoes   person and cut a shallow cross in the top of each potato. Bake at 380° F. or Reg. 5 for 1½ hours.

Apple   2 lb cooking apples   Demerara sugar
Charlotte   Bread and butter   Ground cinnamon

Butter well a deep pie dish or soufflé mould. Peel, core, and slice the apples thinly. Take some sliced white bread and butter it generously. Put the bread and butter and sliced apples into the dish in alternate layers, sprinkling each layer of apples with 3 tablespoons of brown sugar and ½ teaspoon of cinnamon. Finish with a layer of bread and butter. Bake at 380° F. or Reg. 5 for about 45 minutes until the top is deep golden brown and very crisp. Serve warm with cream.

Shopping List

1 large Spanish onion	½ lb tongue
1 lb carrots	¼ lb Italian salami
1 lb leeks	¼ lb kassler
1 lb chicory	¾ lb liver sausage
1 lb beetroot	1 packet pasta
2 lb cooking apples	1 small tin tomatoes
1 bunch watercress	1 packet red kidney beans
or parsley	Parmesan cheese
6 large potatoes	3 bouillon cubes
½ lb ham	½ pt double cream

MENU 17 *Winter Dinner*

Escargots

Chicken with Tarragon

Potatoes with Cream

Lettuce and Cucumber Salad

Poached Oranges with Cointreau

Escargots   6 or 12 escargots per person   Garlic butter
(snails to you)   (depending on capacity)

If you have never had the courage to try escargots and you like garlic, please try them just once. For garlic-eaters they are utterly delicious.

The tinned snails which are obtainable nearly everywhere are very good indeed, but if you have a shop near you which sells ready prepared fresh snails, as many of them do these days, then you can forget the garlic butter and just put them in the oven for the required cooking time.

Put the snails into their shells and fill the shells to the brim with garlic butter. Place them on fireproof plates or dimpled snail dishes and cook in a very hot oven, 425° F. or Reg. 7, for 10 minutes. Serve with French bread.

GARLIC BUTTER FOR 3 DOZEN SNAILS

$\frac{1}{2}$ lb butter   3 cloves garlic
3 tablespoons chopped parsley   Salt and pepper

Cream the butter, and add the parsley and the garlic finely crushed under the blade of a knife (or better still, put through a garlic

44

press). Mix well, add a good pinch of salt and about a half-teaspoon of freshly ground pepper. Mix well again.

Garlic butter goes sour very quickly so it must be eaten on the day you have prepared it.

Chicken with Tarragon

1 large roasting chicken	Salt and black pepper
3 oz butter	2 tablespoons Brandy
2 tablespoons freshly chopped tarragon (or one tablespoon dried tarragon)	4 tablespoons water

Cream 1½ oz of butter with chopped tarragon and salt and pepper. Put inside the bird. Lay the bird on its side and roast until cooked at 400° F. or Reg. 5, basting every 10 minutes and turning the bird over on to its other side at half time. Put the bird on to a dish, carefully drain all the juices out of its inside and keep warm for at least 15 minutes before carving (dish it up before you sit down to your first course and it will be just right).

Add the Brandy and water to the remaining juices in the meat tin and stir well to get all the bits from the bottom and sides of the tin. Bring to the boil fiercely and bubble for 2 minutes and serve in a sauceboat instead of gravy. Please try this; it's much nicer (and easier) than fiddling about with gravy browning and cabbage water!

Potatoes with Cream

1 medium-sized potato per person	½ pt single cream
	Salt and pepper

Peel the potatoes and cut into thin slices about the thickness of a penny. Put into a bowl of cold water and wash well to get rid of the excess starch. Dry on a clean tea towel. Lay in a deep fireproof dish and sprinkle with salt and pepper. Pour the cream over and cook in a medium oven (400° F. or Reg. 5) for 1 hour. This can cook at the same time as the chicken.

Lettuce and Cucumber Salad

As for Menu 3, page 11.

45

Poached Oranges with Cointreau

6 large seedless oranges
8 oz sugar

$\frac{1}{4}$ pt water
2 tablespoons Cointreau

Peel the oranges carefully with a sharp knife taking off all the white pith. Bring the water and sugar to the boil in a shallow pan large enough to take all the oranges together in one layer. As soon as the sugar has melted, turn the heat down low. Just keep the syrup simmering gently. Put in the oranges and poach for 8 minutes. Then turn over and poach for a further 8 minutes on the other side. Take out the oranges and put on to a dish. Bring the syrup back to the boil and cook steadily until it starts to thicken. Add the Cointreau and pour over the oranges. Serve cold. This keeps for a couple of days in the fridge without harm.

Shopping List

1 large roasting chicken
1 bunch parsley
1 lettuce
1 cucumber
6 medium-sized potatoes
6 large seedless oranges
Tarragon (fresh or dried)

3 dozen escargots (tinned will do)
1 lb butter
$\frac{1}{2}$ pt single cream
1 French loaf
1 miniature bottle of Cointreau
Brandy

Crab and Celeriac Salad

Roast Ducklings

Roast Potatoes

Orange Salad

Brandied Crème Brûlée

Crab and Celeriac Salad

1 large head celeriac
½ pt home-made mayonnaise
  (recipe on page 138)
Lettuce, Tomatoes
Chopped parsley

½ lb white crab meat (fresh, tinned, or frozen, it does not matter, but it *must* be white; Russian is very good but rather expensive)

Peel the celeriac and shred into fine matchsticks; this is easy on a mandoline, or universal slicer, as it is sometimes called (see Glossary, page 140). Drop the celeriac into a bowl of cold water which has had two tablespoons of vinegar added to it (this is important otherwise the celeriac will go black if it is exposed to the air). Flake the crab meat into a bowl. Drain and dry the celeriac and mix it into the crab. Add the mayonnaise and blend well together. Serve in a mound on a flat dish surrounded by shredded lettuce and garnished with a few slices of tomato.

Sprinkle with a little chopped parsley and serve with brown bread and butter.

Roast Ducklings

2 ducklings

Salt and pepper

For six people 2 ducklings are necessary. You will have a bit left over, but this is all to the good as duckling is even better cold.

Have the ducks very thoroughly cleaned and defeathered. Make sure there are no quills left in the wings. Rub a mixture of salt and

47

pepper well into the skins and prick them thoroughly all over with a carving fork. Add no fat of any kind. Stand them on a grid in a roasting pan and roast fairly slowly at 380° F. or Reg. 5 for 20 minutes to the pound, pouring off the fat in the roasting tin from time to time. Turn up the heat to 425° F. or Reg. 7 for the last half-hour.

Do not baste during the early part of the roasting, but baste when you turn the oven up and twice more during the last half-hour. Cooked this way, the ducklings will not be at all greasy, and the skins will be beautifully crisp. Do not serve any gravy with them; they taste much better without. Let them rest in the oven with the heat turned off for at least 15–20 minutes. Dish up before you start the first course. They will be just right.

One of the best things about roast duck is the dripping. It makes the most delicious fried bread and sauté potatoes in the world.

Roast Potatoes Peel the required number of potatoes. Cut them into halves or even quarters if they are too big. Put them into a saucepan and cover with cold water. Add 1 tablespoon of salt and bring to the boil. Boil gently for 5 minutes. Drain them and put them into a warm roasting tin covered to half an inch with melted dripping. Turn the potatoes in the dripping until they are well coated. Roast for $1\frac{1}{2}$ hours. They can be put into the oven with the ducklings quite happily.

| Orange Salad | 4 oranges
1 bunch watercress
1 dessertspoon caster sugar | French dressing (recipe on page 137) |

Wash and pick over the watercress making sure there are no dead leaves. Lay on a flat dish. Peel the oranges with a sharp knife taking care to remove all the white pith and slice thinly. Arrange in circles on the dish leaving an edging of watercress leaves round the rim. Sprinkle with French dressing, with 1 dessertspoon of caster sugar added. Serve very cold. This can be prepared 2 hours in advance.

| Brandied
Crème Brûlée | 1 pt single cream
6 egg yolks
6 oz caster sugar | 4 tablespoons Brandy
2 oz Demerara sugar |

Scald the cream (see Glossary, page 141). Beat the egg yolks with the caster sugar and the Brandy until pale. Add the hot cream slowly, beating constantly. Bake in a fireproof dish standing in a baking tin of water in a slow oven at 300° F. or Reg. 2 until set. Leave to cool.

Sprinkle the top with the Demerara sugar, put under a hot grill, and brown carefully. Make sure the sugar does not burn, but it must caramelize (see Glossary, page 140). Refrigerate for at least 4 hours.

| Shopping List | 2 medium-sized ducks
1 large tin white crab meat
(or $\frac{1}{2}$ lb frozen crab meat)
1 large head celeriac
2 lb potatoes | 4 oranges
1 bunch watercress
6 eggs
1 pt single cream
1 miniature bottle of Brandy |

Pâté Maison

Turbot Provençal

Steamed Potatoes

Lettuce Salad

Pineapple with Kirsch

Pâté Maison

1 lb pigs' liver	1 tablespoon salt
1 lb belly of pork	1 teaspoon black pepper
1 lb pie-veal	1 clove of garlic
2 tablespoons Brandy	6 juniper berries
1 wineglass dry Vermouth	Bay leaves

Mince all the meats together. Mince the garlic and the juniper berries in a parsley chopper, or crush in a pestle and mortar (see Glossary, page 141), and add to the meats, together with everything else. Mix very well indeed. Put into one very large or several small terrines. Lay one or two bay leaves on the top and stand the pâté or pâtés in a roasting tin containing an inch of water and bake in the oven at 335° F. or Reg. 3 until the mixture shrinks away from the sides of the dish. Take out of the oven and cool slightly, then put a plate or dish of some kind on the top and weight it. Allow to become quite cold under the weight and then store in the fridge.

Obviously this makes quite a large quantity of pâté but it keeps well for at least a week in the fridge. However, if you only want enough for about 6 people make half quantities.

Turbot Provençal

2 lb turbot	Chopped parsley
1 Spanish onion	Oil, salt, and pepper
1 medium tin tomatoes	Slices of white bread
2 cloves garlic	

Skin and bone the fish and cut into cubes of 1 inch. Heat 3 table-spoons of oil gently in a large frying pan; add the onion, thinly sliced, and the garlic, finely chopped, and fry until golden. Add the fish and continue cooking at the same speed until the fish is opaque; then add the tomatoes, salt, and pepper. Cook slowly until the fish is tender. While the fish is cooking, prepare triangles of bread fried in oil, and keep warm in the oven. Sprinkle the fish with a generous handful of chopped parsley and serve with the triangles of bread.

Steamed Potatoes Peel the potatoes. Cover with salted cold water, bring to the boil, and cook on a medium heat for 10 minutes. Drain. Put in a metal colander over a saucepan with some hot water in it. Put the sauce-pan lid on top of the colander. Place the whole contraption over a medium heat and steam the potatoes until tender.

Lettuce Salad   As for Menu 9, see pages 26 and 11.

Pineapple with Kirsch	1 large pineapple Kirsch	Caster sugar

Take a fine, large, ripe pineapple. Peel thoroughly. Cut into thin slices (take out the hard woody centre of the slices with an apple corer). Arrange on a large dish. Sprinkle each slice with 1 teaspoon of caster sugar and 1 teaspoon of Kirsch. Serve very cold.

Shopping List		
	1 lb pigs' liver	2 lettuces
	1 lb belly of pork	1 pineapple
	1 lb pie-veal	Juniper berries
	2 lb turbot	1 medium tin tomatoes
	1 Spanish onion	1 miniature bottle of Kirsch
	1 bunch parsley	Brandy
	2 lb potatoes	Vermouth

MENU 20 *Winter Dinner*

Individual Cheese Soufflés

Osso Bucco

Risotto Milanese

Chicory Salad

Syllabub

Individual Cheese Soufflés

2 oz butter	4 oz grated Cheddar cheese
2 level tablespoons flour	1 teaspoon Worcester sauce
$\frac{1}{2}$ pt milk	2 egg yolks
Salt and pepper	4 egg whites

Butter 6 individual soufflé dishes. Make a white sauce (recipe on page 139) with the butter, flour, and milk. You must make sure that it is absolutely smooth. Add the cheese, Worcester sauce, salt, and pepper. Continue cooking gently, stirring constantly, until the cheese is melted. Stir in the 2 egg yolks. Cool slightly. Whisk the 4 egg whites until stiff, but not dry, and add to the mixture. Bake at 350° F. or Reg. 4 for 20 minutes. Serve at once.

The cheese mixture can be made ahead of time and the egg whites added at the last moment before baking.

Osso Bucco

6 large slices veal knuckle cut across and through the bone (most good butchers are familiar with this dish now and will know what to give you if you explain what it is for)	2 oz butter
	1 medium tin tomatoes
	1 medium tin petits pois
	1 teacup white wine or dry Vermouth
	Salt and pepper
	A little flour
1 large Spanish onion	

GARNISH

The peel of 1 lemon (peeled very thinly without the white pith)	1 clove garlic
	1 stick celery
	Handful parsley

Roll each piece of meat in flour. Melt the butter in a large frying pan and fry the pieces of meat gently on both sides until golden. Take the meat out and lay it in a casserole. Sprinkle well with salt and pepper. In the remaining butter in the frying pan fry the sliced onion until soft, add the tomatoes, the drained petits pois, and the white wine or Vermouth. Bring the whole mixture to the boil. Pour the whole panful over the meat in the casserole and place the casserole, uncovered, in a slow oven, 335° F. or Reg. 3, for about 2–2½ hours. Finely chop the lemon peel, garlic, celery, and parsley. Mix together. Fifteen minutes before serving, strew the mixture over the top of the meat and put the casserole back in the oven.

This dish is, if anything, better reheated, and it can be made the day before. It can also be left in a low oven for a long time without harm. Do not miss the marrow in the centre of the bone as it is most delicious. Osso bucco is always served with risotto Milanese.

Risotto Milanese

1 Spanish onion	2 envelopes saffron
12 oz Italian rice	Salt and pepper
2 oz butter	Parmesan cheese
1½ pt stock	

Dissolve the saffron in a teacup of hot stock and leave to stand for 5 minutes.

Chop the onion and cook in the butter in a frying pan until the onion is clear. Add the rice and fry gently for 2 minutes. Add the saffron stock and enough plain stock to cover the rice. Cook gently, stirring from time to time until the rice is cooked. Add stock as it is needed. When it is finished the rice should be moist (but not sloppy) and cooked right through. It is difficult to give exact amounts of stock as some rice will absorb more liquid than others.

Season and serve with grated Parmesan cheese.

53

Chicory Salad   1½ lb chicory   Sweet French dressing

Wipe the chicory and slice into chunks with a stainless steel knife. Dress with sweet French dressing (recipe on page 137).

Syllabub   1 orange   2 fluid oz Kirsch
               4 fluid oz Sherry   ½ pt double cream
               4 oz caster sugar

Peel the skin of the orange thinly with a potato peeler or a sharp, stainless steel knife leaving out all the white pith. Put the peel in a bowl and cover with the juice from the orange and the Sherry. Leave 24 hours. Strain into a deep bowl. Stir in the sugar and Kirsch until dissolved. Add the cream slowly and whip until thick (this takes quite a long time). Put into wineglasses and leave at least a day in a cold place before serving.

Shopping List   6 slices veal knuckle (cut   1 lb Italian rice
                  across and through the bone)   2 bouillon cubes
                  2 Spanish onions   2 envelopes saffron
                  1 lemon   Parmesan cheese
                  Celery   ½ pt double cream
                  Parsley   4 oz Cheddar cheese
                  1½ lb chicory   Dry Vermouth or white wine
                  1 orange   1 miniature bottle of Kirsch
                  1 medium tin tomatoes   Sherry
                  1 medium tin petits pois

MENU 21 *Winter Dinner*

Hors d'Œuvre: Carrot Salad

Tomato Salad

Egg Mayonnaise

Bœuf Bourguignonne

Steamed Potatoes

Lettuce Salad

Pot Chocolat

Hors d'Œuvre: Obviously a mixed hors d'œuvre can consist of as many different dishes as you please, but I find that three, or at the most four, dishes are enough to cope with at home. In each case where I have recommended hors d'œuvre as a first course, I have given a small selection which blend well.

Carrot Salad

1 lb large carrots
Sweetened French dressing (recipe on page 137)

Peel and grate the carrots fairly coarsely. Sprinkle with slightly sweetened French dressing.

Tomato Salad

1 lb tomatoes
1 small onion
Chopped parsley
French dressing (recipe on page 137)

Slice the tomatoes and lay on a flat dish. Thinly slice the onion and lay on top of the tomatoes. Sprinkle with French dressing and finely chopped parsley.

Egg	6 eggs	½ pt home-made mayonnaise
Mayonnaise		(recipe on page 138)

Hard boil the eggs. Cool, shell, and cut them into halves lengthwise. Lay cut side down on a flat dish. Put a large spoonful of home-made mayonnaise on each half. (Please do not use the bottled kind of mayonnaise with this dish; it tastes quite revolting!) Leave for at least half an hour before eating.

Bœuf	2½ lb lean top rump of beef	½ lb baby onions
Bourguig-	(cut into 1-inch cubes)	A little flour
nonne	¼ lb streaky bacon (diced small)	Butter
		1 pt red wine
	½ lb mushrooms (quartered)	Salt and pepper
	1 large onion	Bay leaf

Toss the meat lightly in flour and shake off the excess. Melt a lump of butter in a frying pan and add the bacon. Fry until the fat begins to run. Add the meat and brown lightly all over. Take out the meat and bacon and put them into a casserole. Fry the onion, finely chopped, in the remaining fat until soft. Add the red wine, seasoning, and bay leaf and bring to the boil. Pour over the meat. Cook uncovered in a low oven, 335° F. or Reg. 3, for 2 hours. After 1½ hours add the peeled baby onions and the mushrooms and mix in well; continue cooking for the remaining half-hour. Serve straight from the casserole. This reheats well.

56

Steamed Potatoes	Cook as for Menu 19, see page 51.
Lettuce Salad	As for Menu 9, see pages 26 and 11.

Pot Chocolat   4 oz plain chocolate   2 tablespoons strong black
                4 eggs   coffee (fresh, not instant)

Break the chocolate into pieces and put in a basin with the black coffee. Put the basin over a saucepan of hot water and melt until completely soft. Separate the eggs and add the yolks to the chocolate one by one, beating well after adding each yolk. Whisk the egg whites until stiff. Fold the chocolate mixture into the egg whites and blend lightly but thoroughly. Pour into small pots or glasses and refrigerate at least 4 hours. It keeps in the fridge for several days.

Shopping List

2½ lb lean top rump of beef	2 lb potatoes
1 lb large carrots	2 lettuces
1 lb tomatoes	¼ lb streaky bacon
½ lb onions	Fresh ground coffee
Parsley	4 oz plain chocolate
½ lb mushrooms	10 eggs
½ lb baby onions	½ bottle red wine

MENU 22 *Winter Dinner*

Leek and Potato Soup

Roast Lamb with Garlic

Flageolet Beans

Iced Lemon Soufflé

Leek and Potato Soup

1 lb leeks	3 pt stock or water
1 lb potatoes	Salt and pepper
1 onion	Chopped parsley
2 oz butter	$\frac{1}{4}$ pt single cream

Wash, peel, and slice the potatoes; chop the onion; clean and slice the leeks leaving on as much green as possible. Melt the butter in a large saucepan, add the vegetables, cover and cook gently for 10 minutes. Add the salt, pepper, and stock. Bring to the boil and simmer gently, uncovered, until the vegetables are very soft. Put the whole mixture through a sieve, Mouli, or blender, whichever you have (a blender is, of course, the easiest). When it is quite smooth put into a clean saucepan, taste, and adjust seasoning. Add cream and a handful of chopped parsley. Reheat slowly until just boiling. This soup comes out a beautiful pale green. It can be made in the morning and reheated at night without deteriorating in any way.

Roast Lamb with Garlic

Leg or loin of lamb	Butter
4 cloves garlic	Salt and pepper

Take a leg or loin of lamb. Cut little pockets near to the bone with a small sharp knife. Put a piece of garlic in each pocket. Rub the skin well with salt and pepper and spread lightly with softened butter. Roast as you usually do but be sure not to over-cook. It should have a touch of pink when it is carved.

Serve the meat in a deep dish surrounded by the flageolet beans so that the juices mingle when the meat is cut.

Flageolet Beans	2 tins French flageolet beans Butter	Salt and pepper

Two tins of flageolet beans are enough for six as they are very filling. Heat the beans with their liquid, seasoning, and a lump of butter until they are very hot.

Iced Lemon Soufflé	3 eggs 4 oz sugar $\frac{1}{2}$ oz gelatine	$\frac{1}{2}$ pt double cream (whipped) $\frac{1}{4}$ pt fresh lemon juice Grated peel of a lemon

Separate the egg yolks from the whites. Whip the whites until stiff and set aside. Soak the gelatine in the lemon juice and heat over hot water until melted. Whisk the egg yolks and sugar together over hot water until thick. Add the gelatine, whipped cream, lemon peel, and finally fold in the egg whites. Pour into a soufflé dish or glass bowl and refrigerate for at least 4 hours. Garnish as you please, i.e. whipped cream and angelica.

Shopping List	1 leg or loin of lamb 1 lb leeks 1 lb potatoes 1 onion Parsley 3 lemons	2 tins French flageolet beans 2 bouillon cubes Gelatine $\frac{1}{4}$ pt single cream $\frac{1}{2}$ pt double cream

MENU 23 *Winter Dinner*

Soup Perisioare

Fish Ritz

New Potatoes, Lettuce Salad

Pears Melba

This soup is Romanian and very original and delicious.

Soup
Perisioare

1 lb tomatoes
½ lb minced beef
1 lb potatoes
1 clove garlic
2 oz butter
½ lb leeks
1 tablespoon finely chopped
  onion

1 tablespoon finely chopped
  parsley
Salt and pepper
3 pt stock (home-made)
¼ pt sour cream
3 bay leaves
1 egg yolk

Skin the tomatoes, clean the leeks, and peel the potatoes. Chop them into rough chunks. Melt the butter in a fairly large saucepan. Put in the chopped garlic, tomatoes, leeks, potatoes, and bay leaves. Sweat (see Glossary, page 141) for 10 minutes with the lid on. Pour on the stock and bring to the boil. Add salt and pepper and cook steadily, uncovered, until all the vegetables are soft. Take out the bay leaves and sieve or purée the whole saucepanful (it should be fairly thin). Mix together the minced beef, finely chopped onion and parsley, and the egg yolk. Add salt and pepper. Form into very tiny hamburgers. Bring the soup to the boil, add the hamburgers and simmer, covered, until the hamburgers are cooked, for about 10–15 minutes.

Serve in cups with a good dollop of sour cream.

Fish Ritz	12 fillets of sole or 6 slices of turbot or halibut	$\frac{1}{4}$ lb mushrooms
	1 wineglass dry Vermouth	$\frac{1}{4}$ lb shrimps or prawns
	2 bay leaves	Butter
	$\frac{1}{2}$ lemon	1 tablespoon flour
	Sprig of parsley	$\frac{1}{2}$ pt single cream
	1 small onion	Pepper and salt

Slice the mushrooms very thinly and cook in 1 oz butter; set aside.

Put the fish into a baking tin, cover with the sliced onion, the sliced lemon, 2 bay leaves, parsley, salt and pepper, and Vermouth. Cover with buttered paper and cook at 335° F. or Reg. 3 for half an hour. Drain the fish well, reserving the liquor, and lay in a fireproof dish. Strew the shrimps and mushrooms over the top and cover with the sauce. Reheat in a slow oven when needed.

SAUCE
Melt 1 oz butter in a saucepan. Add the flour, mix well, and cook gently for 2 minutes. Add the strained fish liquor gradually, stirring thoroughly. Bring to the boil and simmer gently for 10 minutes, stirring constantly. Add the cream. Bring to boiling point again and pour over the fish.

New Potatoes Heat 2 tins new potatoes in a metal colander over hot water until they are hot right through. This takes about 10 minutes.

Lettuce Salad As for Menu 9, see pages 26 and 11.

Pears Melba

6 large unripe pears	3 drops cochineal
8 oz sugar	1 packet frozen unsugared
$\frac{1}{4}$ pt water	strawberries

Put the sugar, water, and cochineal in a shallow pan and bring to the boil, stirring to dissolve the sugar. Boil gently for 5 minutes. Peel the pears thinly, leaving them whole and with the stalks on. Poach the pears gently in the syrup until they are tender, but not mushy. Take them out and put in a dish. Put the defrosted strawberries into the syrup and cook until they are very soft. Sieve or purée the strawberries and syrup. Pour over the pears and leave to get very cold.

You can serve this with ice cream or whipped cream.

Shopping List

12 fillets of sole or 6 slices of turbot or halibut	2 lettuces
$\frac{1}{4}$ lb shrimps or prawns	6 large unripe pears
$\frac{1}{2}$ lb minced beef	2 large tins new potatoes
1 lb tomatoes	Cochineal
$\frac{1}{2}$ lb leeks	1 packet frozen unsugared strawberries
1 lb potatoes	1 block ice cream (or $\frac{1}{2}$ pt double cream)
Parsley	
$\frac{1}{2}$ lb onions	$\frac{1}{2}$ pt single cream
1 lemon	$\frac{1}{4}$ pt sour cream
$\frac{1}{4}$ lb mushrooms	Dry Vermouth

MENU 24 *Winter Dinner*

Salmon Mousse

Lamb Cutlets

Jacket Potatoes

Cole Slaw

Apple Flan

Salmon Mousse	1 large tin of salmon ½ pt thick béchamel (recipe on page 139)	1 tablespoon dry Sherry ¼ pt double cream (whipped)

Mash the salmon into a very smooth paste (you can put it in a blender if you have one) and add the béchamel, Sherry, and the whipped cream. Blend well. Pour into a dish or bowl and refrigerate at least 6 hours.

Lamb Cutlets	12 lamb cutlets Salt and pepper	1 oz butter

Melt the butter and fry the seasoned cutlets until just browned. Put into a baking tin and pour over the liquid from the frying pan. Put in the oven, 350° F. or Reg. 4, for half an hour, turning over at half time. This is a much easier and better way of cooking any kind of chops as they cook through without becoming burnt or dry.

Jacket Potatoes As for Menu 16, see page 43.

63

Cole Slaw

½ Dutch white cabbage
½ lb carrots
1 eating apple

½ pt home-made mayonnaise
(recipe on p. 138)
Chopped parsley

Cut the stump out of the cabbage and shred finely. Peel and grate the carrots coarsely. Peel the apple and cut into matchsticks. Mix all together. Pour the mayonnaise over. Blend all together very well. Serve in a mound on a flat dish sprinkled with a little chopped parsley.

Apple Flan

½ lb shortcrust pastry
2 large cooking apples
4 oz caster sugar

3 tablespoons apricot jam
4 tablespoons water

Line a flan tin with shortcrust pastry and bake blind (see Glossary, page 140) until just set but not coloured (about 10 minutes at 400° F. or Reg. 5). Cool. Peel and slice one apple thinly and cook in a saucepan with 3 oz caster sugar and 2 tablespoons water until it is a thick purée. Cool and pour into the flan case. Peel the other apple and slice thinly and lay evenly in neat circles in the flan case. Sprinkle with the remaining ounce of sugar and bake at 335° F. or Reg. 3 until the apple slices are tender and just beginning to brown at the edges. Heat the apricot jam and 2 tablespoons water together until the jam has melted. Sieve, and spoon gently over the flan making sure the whole flan is glazed. Serve cold.

Shopping List

12 lamb cutlets
6 large potatoes
½ Dutch white cabbage
½ lb carrots
2 large cooking apples
1 large eating apple

Parsley
1 large tin of salmon
1 small pot apricot jam
½ lb shortcrust pastry
¼ pt double cream
Sherry

Tomatoes in Cream

Roast Loin of Pork with Wine Gravy

Purée Potatoes, Chicory and Beetroot Salad

Baked Apricots

Tomatoes in Cream

12 large tomatoes
2 oz butter
Salt and pepper

½ pt single cream
Large handful chopped parsley

Cut the tomatoes in halves. Melt the butter in a large frying pan. Fry the tomatoes on both sides until browned. Put into a fireproof dish, season with salt and pepper, and keep warm. Pour the cream and parsley into the frying pan and bring to the boil. Pour over the tomatoes.

Serve with lots of French bread.

Roast Loin of Pork with Wine Gravy

5 lb loin of pork
Salt and pepper

½ pt red wine

Get your butcher to bone a loin of pork weighing about 5 lb and tie it into a neat roll. This way there will be no waste and it will be easy to carve. Salt and pepper the joint and roast it gently at 335° F. or Reg. 3 for 2 hours without basting, then baste and turn the oven up to 425° F. or Reg. 7 and roast for half an hour more. Allow the joint to rest in a warm oven for 15–20 minutes before carving.

WINE GRAVY
Pour the fat off the roasting tin gently so that the essence is left behind. Pour ½ pint red wine into the tin and bring to the boil, allowing to bubble for a few minutes. Serve in a separate sauce-boat.

Purée Potatoes	As for Menu 2, see page 7.

Chicory and Beetroot Salad	As for Menu 2, see page 7.

Baked Apricots

2 lb apricots	3 oz vanilla sugar (recipe on page 139)
2 tablespoons water	2 tablespoons Cointreau or Kirsch

Wash and dry the apricots. Make a small incision in the side of each one in the natural crease of the fruit. Sprinkle the water into a fireproof dish and put all the apricots in it in one layer. Sprinkle with the sugar and the liqueur. Bake in a slow oven, 300° F. or Reg. 2, until they are tender, turning over after 20 minutes. Take out the apricots with a slotted spoon and put into a serving dish. Bring the juices in the cooking dish to the boil and simmer until they start to thicken.

Pour over the apricots and serve very cold with thick cream.

Shopping List

5 lb loin of pork	$\frac{1}{2}$ pt single cream
Parsley	$\frac{1}{2}$ pt double cream
2 lb potatoes	French bread
2 lb apricots	$\frac{1}{2}$ bottle red wine
1 lb chicory	1 miniature bottle of
1 lb beetroot	Cointreau or Kirsch
12 large tomatoes	

66

MENU 26 *Winter Dinner*

Hors d'Œuvre: Cauliflower Vinaigrette

Tunny Fish with Onion

Radishes

Chicken Souvaroff

New Potatoes

Lettuce and Cucumber Salad

Peach Soufflé

Hors d'Œuvre: Cauliflower Vinaigrette	1 cauliflower Chopped parsley	French dressing (recipe on page 137)

Clean the cauliflower and cut off the leaves. Put into a metal colander and steam over a saucepan of boiling water until it is tender. Put into a serving dish and pour French dressing over it while it is still hot. Allow to cool. When quite cold sprinkle with chopped parsley.

Tunny Fish with Onion	2 tins tunny fish $\frac{1}{2}$ Spanish onion	$\frac{1}{4}$ pt mayonnaise (recipe on page 138)

Drain the tunny fish and flake into a bowl. Add the home-made mayonnaise and mix lightly. Put into a flat serving dish and cover with the onion cut into the thinnest possible slices.

Radishes At least two bunches cleaned and washed with a little of the green left on.

Chicken Souvaroff	2 2½-lb chickens	4 tablespoons white wine
	8 oz liver pâté	Butter
	3 tablespoons Brandy	Salt and pepper
	4 tablespoons Madeira or Sherry	

Mash the liver pâté with 1 tablespoon Brandy and stuff the chickens with this mixture (the pâté is obtainable at most good delicatessen shops and costs about 3s. a quarter for the truffled kind, which is the best). Spread the breasts of the chickens with soft butter and salt and pepper them. Roast in a medium oven, 380° F. or Reg. 5, for 40 minutes. Carve the chickens into portions without taking them out of the roasting tin (in this way none of the juice or stuffing is lost). Put the pieces of chicken into a casserole. Put the rest of the Brandy, the Madeira (or Sherry), and the white wine into the roasting tin and bring to the boil. Scrape up all the bits and pieces adhering to the tin and pour the lot over the chicken pieces. Cover and bake in a hot oven, 425° F. or Reg. 7, for 20 minutes.

Do not under any circumstances remove the lid until you get the dish into the dining-room, because the scent when it is first uncovered is divine. It must be served straight from the casserole. The first part of the cooking can be done in advance and the final cooking done in the evening.

68

New Potatoes	As for Menu 23, see page 62.
Lettuce and Cucumber Salad	As for Menu 3, see page 11.

Peach Soufflé

1 large tin peaches	1 teaspoon almond essence
3 tablespoons water	2 oz caster sugar
1 oz gelatine	$\frac{1}{2}$ pt double cream
1 tablespoon lemon juice	4 eggs

Soften the gelatine in the water and lemon juice and melt over hot water. Cool.

Drain the peaches, reserving the syrup. Separate the eggs. Whisk the egg yolks and add the peach syrup slowly, beating until thick. Whisk egg whites until stiff, fold in the sugar, and whisk again until shiny. Purée the peaches. Whip the cream. Combine together, the egg yolk mixture, the peach purée, the gelatine, the almond essence, the whipped cream, and finally the egg whites. Mix lightly together and pour into a bowl or soufflé dish. Chill.

This can be made the day before. It entails a lot of washing up but it is very festive and delicious. It is worth the trouble and not too expensive.

Shopping List

2 2½-lb chickens	2 tins new potatoes
1 cauliflower	1 large tin peaches
Parsley	Almond essence
1 Spanish onion	Gelatine
2 bunches radishes	8 oz liver pâté
1 lettuce	$\frac{1}{2}$ pt double cream
1 lemon	Madeira or Sherry
1 cucumber	White wine
2 tins tunny fish	Brandy

MENU 27 *Winter Dinner*

Devilled Crab

Bœuf en Croûte

Pommes de Terre au Beurre

Lettuce and Cucumber Salad

Grand Marnier Ice Cream

Devilled Crab

1 lb white crab meat (fresh, frozen, or tinned)
¼ lb mushrooms
1 Spanish onion
2 oz butter
2 teaspoons tomato purée
1 teacup water
¼ pt double cream
1 tablespoon curry powder
½ teaspoon cayenne pepper
Breadcrumbs

Chop the onion and the mushrooms very fine. Melt 1½ oz butter in a large frying pan. Cook the onion and mushrooms in it until they are soft. Add the crab. Dissolve the tomato purée, curry powder, and cayenne in the water. Add to the pan and simmer for a few minutes until thick. Add the cream. Bring to the boil and cook slowly for a further 5 minutes. Put into 6 individual ramekins or scallop shells. Sprinkle liberally with soft white breadcrumbs and dot with the remaining ½ oz butter divided into 6 small pieces. Cook under a slow grill until hot right through and well browned on the top. Serve with French bread.

Bœuf en Croûte

3 lb contrefilet of beef
1 wineglass of Brandy
1 wineglass of Sherry
1 wineglass Marsala or Madeira
3 bay leaves
10 juniper berries
Salt, black peppercorns
1 lb puff pastry (frozen is very good)
2 teaspoons arrowroot
Cream or beaten egg

Put the beef into a bowl. Rub all over with salt, pour over the Brandy, Sherry, and Marsala or Madeira. Add the bay leaves, juniper berries, and black peppercorns. Cover and leave in a cool place for 24 hours turning occasionally.

Take the meat out of the marinade and dry it, reserving the marinade. Roast in a medium oven, 400° F. or Reg. 5, for 1 hour, basting often. Take out of the meat tin, put on a grid and cool slightly. Do not allow the meat to become cold. Wrap it in puff pastry. Glaze with cream or beaten egg and bake at 425° F. or Reg. 7 until well risen and brown, for about half an hour.

While it is baking strain the marinade into a saucepan. Bring to the boil and thicken slightly with the arrowroot. Serve as a gravy.

**Pommes
de Terre
au Beurre**

| 2 lb potatoes | Salt and pepper |
| 3 oz butter | |

Boil the potatoes in their skins gently for 10 minutes until a fork just pierces the skin easily. Strain. Cool enough to handle, peel, and cut into quarters. Melt the butter in a fireproof dish and turn the potatoes in it until well coated. Bake at 290° F. or Reg. 1 for 2 hours turning every half-hour. Sprinkle with salt and pepper at the moment of service.

**Lettuce and
Cucumber
Salad**

As for Menu 3, see page 11.

Grand	1 pt double cream	$\frac{1}{2}$ pt water
Marnier	4 egg yolks	6 tablespoons Grand Marnier
Ice Cream	6 oz caster sugar	

Dissolve the sugar in the water. Bring to the boil and simmer until it is reduced to $\frac{1}{4}$ pt. Whisk the egg yolks. Pour in the syrup in a steady stream and whip again. Whip the cream until very thick, but not stiff, and add the Grand Marnier. Fold the cream into the egg mixture. Blend well. Turn the refrigerater up to very cold. Pour the ice-cream mixture into freezing trays. Freeze until firm. Serve in glasses (it should not be too hard).

Shopping List	3 lb contrefilet of beef	Arrowroot
	1 lb white crab meat	1 small tin tomato purée
	2 lb potatoes	$1\frac{1}{4}$ pt double cream
	1 lettuce	French bread
	1 cucumber	2 miniature bottles Grand Marnier
	1 Spanish onion	Marsala or Madeira
	$\frac{1}{4}$ lb mushrooms	Brandy
	Juniper berries	Sherry
	1 lb packet frozen puff pastry	

SUMMER
LUNCHEONS
AND FAMILY
SUPPERS

Iced Tomato Consommé

Veal Escalopes à la Crème

Noodles

Tomato and Cucumber Salad

Strawberry Flan

Iced Tomato Consommé	1 beef bone	Salt and peppercorns
	1 lb minced beef	1 onion
	1 lb tomatoes	

Ask the butcher to chop the bone into halves. Put the bones, the minced beef, the washed unpeeled onion and tomatoes, a little salt, and 6 black peppercorns into a large saucepan. Cover with 6 pints of cold water. Bring slowly to the boil, skimming off the scum as it rises. When the surface is free from scum turn down the heat and simmer slowly until the liquid is reduced by half. Put a piece of linen into a colander and pour the soup through it into a clean bowl. Leave in a cold place overnight. Take off every scrap of fat. Ladle the soup, which should be lightly jellied and quite clear, into individual bowls.

Serve with quarters of lemon.

Veal Escalopes à la Crème	6 veal escalopes cut very thin	2 oz butter
	1 lemon	½ pt single cream
	1 tablespoon oil	Salt and pepper

Put the escalopes on to a dish and sprinkle with salt and pepper, and the juice of one lemon. Leave to stand for about 1 hour. Heat the oil and butter in a large frying pan until the butter foams.

74

Put in the escalopes and fry gently until light brown on both sides. Take out the meat and keep warm on a hot dish.

Pour the lemon juice from the dish into the pan and stir well round to dissolve the essence of the meat into the sauce. Boil for one minute. Pour in the cream, heat through, stirring constantly. Pour the coffee-coloured sauce over the meat and serve. This will keep warm while you eat your first course.

Noodles | 1 lb Italian noodles | Salt
2 tablespoons oil

Bring a large saucepan of water to the boil, salt it and add the oil. Put in the noodles, being careful not to break them. Simmer for 8 minutes, stirring occasionally with a fork. Strain through a metal colander. Set the colander over a saucepan containing 2 inches of water. Cover the colander with a saucepan lid and put over a gentle heat. The noodles will keep warm without further cooking while you eat your soup.

Tomato and | 1 lb tomatoes | French dressing (recipe on page 137)
Cucumber | 1 cucumber | Chopped parsley
Salad

Skin the tomatoes and cut into quarters. Peel the cucumber, cut in half lengthwise and take out the seeds by running a teaspoon down the inside of the cucumber. Cut into fairly thick slices. Put the tomatoes and cucumber into a bowl. Pour over the dressing. Toss together. Sprinkle with chopped parsley. Leave to stand in the refrigerator for about an hour.

Strawberry | $\frac{1}{2}$ lb shortcrust pastry | $\frac{1}{2}$ lb redcurrant jelly
Flan | 1 lb strawberries | 4 tablespoons water

Roll out the pastry, not too thin, and line a large flan tin. Bake blind (see Glossary, page 140) until golden brown. Cool. Hull the strawberries, lay neatly in the flan case, covering the bottom completely. Put the redcurrant jelly and the water into a saucepan. Heat gently, stirring, until the jelly is melted. Cool until cold.

Spoon the jelly over the strawberries until they are thickly coated. Leave in a cold place until set.

This must be eaten the same day as it is made, otherwise the pastry goes soggy.

Shopping List

6 veal escalopes
1 lb minced beef
1 beef bone
2 lb tomatoes
1 onion
1 lemon
1 cucumber

Parsley
1 lb strawberries
1 lb Italian noodles
$\frac{1}{2}$ lb shortcrust pastry
$\frac{1}{2}$ lb redcurrant jelly
$\frac{1}{2}$ pt single cream

Aubergines au Gratin

Cold Ham and Salami

Mostarda de Cremona

Jacket Potatoes

Honey Cream

Aubergines
au Gratin

4 large aubergines	1 medium tin of tomatoes
1 Spanish onion	2 tablespoons chopped parsley
2 cloves of garlic	1 teacup soft white
4 tablespoons oil	breadcrumbs
1 oz butter	Salt and pepper

Cut the unpeeled aubergines into thick slices. Fry gently in the oil until golden brown. Take out the aubergines and set aside. Put the chopped onion and the minced garlic into the oil and cook until golden. Add the tomatoes and parsley and cook gently for 5 minutes. Add the aubergines and cook for 2 minutes. Add salt and pepper. Pour the whole mixture into a fairly shallow fireproof dish. Cool. When it is quite cold strew the breadcrumbs on the top and dot with the butter. Bake at 400° F. or Reg. 6 for half an hour.

Cold Ham
and Salami

1½ lb sliced cold ham	¼ lb thinly sliced salami
Watercress	

Arrange the ham and salami neatly on a large dish. Decorate with well washed watercress.

Mostarda   This is a delicious relish to serve with cold ham. It is made with
de Cremona   different fruits preserved in a mustard-flavoured syrup. Not only
does it taste absolutely super, but it looks divine. You can buy it in
large stores and good Italian shops. It is rather expensive but
worth it.

Jacket Potatoes   As for Menu 16, see page 43.

Honey Cream   4 eggs $\frac{1}{2}$-lb jar clear honey
$\frac{3}{4}$ pt double cream

Separate the eggs, whip the yolks until thick, and add the honey
to the eggs beating all the time. Set the bowl with the egg yolks
and honey over a saucepan of hot water. Stir over simmering
water until very thick. Cool. Whisk the egg whites until stiff.
Whip the cream. Fold the egg whites and the whipped cream into
the egg yolks and honey mixture. Put into the coldest part of the
refrigerator for at least 2 hours, but not longer than 4 hours,
otherwise the honey may start to separate from the other ingredients.

Shopping List   4 large aubergines $\frac{1}{4}$ lb Italian salami
1 Spanish onion   Mostarda de Cremona
Parsley   1 medium tin tomatoes
Watercress $\frac{1}{2}$-lb jar clear honey
6 large potatoes $\frac{3}{4}$ pt double cream
$1\frac{1}{2}$ lb sliced ham

Asparagus

Entrecôte Steaks Bearnaise

French Fried Potatoes, Stuffed Tomatoes

Raspberry Trifle

Asparagus   1 Cos lettuce   French dressing (recipe on page 137)
Salad   2½ lb asparagus   Parsley

Wash and dry the lettuce. Separate the leaves and lay on a flat dish. Cook the asparagus as for Menu 6 (see page 18). Cool. Arrange the asparagus on top of the lettuce. Pour French dressing over. Stand in the refrigerator for half an hour. Sprinkle with chopped parsley.

Entrecôte   6 entrecôte steaks weighing about   Oil
Steaks   6 oz each   Salt and pepper

Season the steaks with salt and pepper. Put on a flat dish, and pour over a little oil (about 2 tablespoonfuls). Leave to stand about

an hour. Make your grill as hot as you can and grill the steak
rapidly. If the grill is hot enough they should not take more than
3 minutes on each side.

BÉARNAISE SAUCE

2 shallots	2 egg yolks
2 tablespoons white wine	1 tablespoon chopped tar-
$\frac{1}{2}$ lb butter	ragon (fresh is best but
1 tablespoon chopped parsley	dried will do at a pinch)
2 tablespoons wine vinegar	

Chop the shallots and put in a small saucepan with the vinegar and
the white wine. Bring to the boil. Cook rapidly until the liquid is
reduced to about one tablespoon. Strain the liquid into a bowl, add
the two egg yolks, and stir until well blended. Set the bowl over a
saucepan of hot (but not boiling) water. Divide the butter into
8 pieces. Add the pieces of butter to the egg mixture one by one
stirring all the time. Allow each piece of butter to dissolve before
adding the next one. By the time the butter has all been added the
sauce will be thick. Take the bowl out of the saucepan and add the
tarragon and parsley. Pour into a heated sauceboat. This sauce
should never be hot, it should be served tepid.

The steaks and the sauce can both be cooked before you eat the
asparagus salad. You can keep the steaks warm, but not the sauce.
However, if the sauceboat is heated the sauce will be quite all right.

French Fried Potatoes	2 lb potatoes	Salt	Oil

Peel the potatoes and cut into fairly small, even chips. Put into
bowl of cold water and stand for 10 minutes. Fill a chip pan one
third full of oil (corn oil is good). Heat the oil gently until hot but
not boiling. Dry the chips on a clean cloth. Cook the chips gently
in the oil until they are tender but not coloured (you can prod them
with a fork). Drain them well and allow them to become cold.
This operation can be done earlier in the day. Just before you are
ready to eat, heat the oil until boiling (if a 1-inch square of bread
will brown in one minute the oil is hot enough). Plunge the chips
into the hot oil and cook until brown and crisp. Drain well and salt
lightly. Keep warm with the steaks.

Stuffed
Tomatoes

9 large tomatoes	4 tablespoons rice
1 chopped shallot	2 oz chopped walnuts
1 dessertspoon currants	Grated peel of $\frac{1}{2}$ lemon
Salt and pepper	1 beaten egg
Nutmeg	2 oz butter

Cut the tomatoes in halves. Remove and reserve the pulp, and put into a bowl. Turn the tomato halves upside down to drain. Boil the rice for 12 minutes, drain, and mix with the tomato pulp. Stir in the shallot, walnuts, currants, lemon peel, salt and pepper, and the beaten egg. Mix well. Pile the mixture into the tomato cases. Divide the butter into eighteen little pieces. Put a piece on each tomato half. Bake at 350° F. or Reg. 4 for half an hour.

Raspberry
Trifle

1 lb raspberries	4 oz sugar
4 tablespoons Kirsch	1 sponge cake
$\frac{1}{2}$ pt whipped cream	

Mix the raspberries, sugar, and Kirsch together. Leave to stand for 6 hours. Line a fairly shallow serving dish with sponge cake. Pour the raspberries and their juice into the dish. Cover with more sponge cake. Set a plate on top and a weight on top of the plate. Leave overnight. Half an hour before serving remove the plate and cover the top with the whipped cream.

Shopping List

6 entrecôte steaks	2 oz shelled walnuts
$\frac{1}{4}$ lb shallots	1 plain sponge cake (home made is best if you can be bothered)
2 lb potatoes	
9 large tomatoes	
1 lemon	Wine vinegar
1 Cos lettuce	$\frac{1}{2}$ lb butter
$2\frac{1}{2}$ lb asparagus	$\frac{1}{2}$ pt double cream
Parsley	White wine
1 lb raspberries	1 miniature bottle of Kirsch
Tarragon (fresh or dried)	

MENU 31 *Summer Luncheon*

Hors d'Œuvre: Lentil Salad

Rollmops

Radishes

Fruit Mayonnaise

Double Lamb Cutlets

French Beans, New Potatoes

Meringues with Walnuts

Hors d'Œuvre: Lentil Salad

$\frac{1}{2}$ lb red or green lentils
2 tablespoons oil
1 Spanish onion
2 bay leaves

2 teaspoons salt
French dressing (recipe on page 137)
3 pt water

Cover the lentils with cold water and soak overnight. Chop the onion, and cook in the oil in a saucepan until it is soft but not browned. Add salt and bay leaves and 3 pints of water. Bring to the boil. Add the drained lentils and simmer until the lentils are tender but not mushy. Drain well. Mix with 4 tablespoons of French dressing and cool. This can be made the day before and left in the fridge overnight. In this case cover the dish with tinfoil when it has become cold.

Rollmops The delicatessen ones are very good and it is such a performance to make them at home that I never bother. Buy one whole piece for each person. No one ever eats two.

Radishes   As for Menu 26, see page 67.

Fruit   3 eating apples $\frac{1}{2}$ pt home-made mayonnaise
Mayonnaise 2 oranges   (recipe on page 138)
              2 bananas

This sounds outlandish but it is, in fact, excellent and it offsets the soft sharp taste of the rollmops perfectly as it is slightly sweet and crisp.

Peel, core, and dice the apples. Peel the oranges very carefully. Cut the flesh away from the membrane and cut into pieces. Dice the bananas. Mix all the fruits together with the mayonnaise and serve very cold.

This must be eaten the same day as it is made otherwise the apple will go soft.

Double Lamb   6 large double lamb cutlets   Salt, pepper
Cutlets   2 oz butter

Melt the butter and fry the chops until light brown on both sides. Put the chops into a roasting tin. Season with salt and pepper. Pour over the fat and juices from the frying pan. Put into a medium oven, 350° F. or Reg. 4, for half an hour turning the chops over at half time.

83

French Beans   2 lb French beans   Salt and pepper
1 oz butter

Top and tail the beans. Drop into boiling salted water. Turn down the heat and simmer until tender. Drain and cool. Melt the butter and toss the beans in it until they are very hot, and shiny.

New Potatoes   Cook as for Menu 6, see page 19.

Meringues   4 egg whites $\frac{1}{2}$ pt double cream
with Walnuts 14 tablespoons caster sugar   4 oz walnuts

Whisk the egg whites until stiff. Add 9 tablespoons sugar. Whisk again until the mixture is thick, shiny, and stiff. Fold the remaining 5 tablespoons of sugar lightly into mixture. Brush baking sheets with vegetable oil. Spoon the mixture on to the sheets with a large tablespoon. You should have 12 equal-sized dollops. Bake at 200° F. or Reg. 2 for 2 hours, turning them over after 1 hour to dry out thoroughly. Cool on a wire grid. Whisk the cream until thick and fold in the walnuts. Put the meringues together in pairs with a generous amount of whipped cream between them.

These can be made several days before and kept in a tin, providing you do not put in the cream filling until about an hour before you eat.

Shopping List   6 double lamb cutlets   2 lb new potatoes
1 Spanish onion $\frac{1}{2}$ lb red or green lentils
1 bunch radishes   4 oz shelled walnuts
1 lb apples   6 rollmops
2 oranges   Caster sugar
2 bananas   6 eggs
2 lb French beans $\frac{1}{2}$ pt double cream

MENU 32 *Summer Family Supper*

Sole Florentine

New Potatoes

Fresh Peaches

Sole 18 fillets of sole
Florentine 3 $\frac{1}{2}$-lb packets frozen leaf
spinach (lazy but much less
trouble)
4 oz butter

1 tablespoon flour
1 pt milk
4 oz grated cheese
Salt and pepper

Put the fish into a baking tin and cover with milk. Set in a medium
oven, 350° F. or Reg. 4, for 15 minutes. Take out the fish and
drain. Strain and reserve the milk. Cook the spinach gently with 1 oz
of butter until tender and dry. Season it and lay in a large buttered
fireproof dish. Arrange the fish neatly on top of the spinach.

Melt 2 oz of butter in a saucepan, add the flour, and blend in the
milk. Bring to the boil and simmer for 10 minutes, stirring constantly. Add 3 oz of grated cheese and stir until the cheese has
melted. Season the sauce lightly. Pour it over the fish and spinach.
Sprinkle with the remaining ounce of cheese and dot with the
remaining ounce of butter. Bake in a medium oven, 350° F. or
Reg. 4, for 20 minutes until brown and bubbly on the top.

Serve at once with lots of new potatoes.

This can be made well ahead of time up to the point where it is
to be put into the oven. Make it in the morning or when you will,
and just put it in the oven 20 minutes before you want to eat.

Fresh Peaches Ripe peaches
Lemon juice

Sugar
$\frac{1}{2}$ pt double cream

Take as many fresh ripe peaches as you can afford. Peel them, dip
them in lemon juice then in caster sugar. Serve with lots of thick
cream. Delicious!

85

Shopping List

18 fillets of sole
2 lb new potatoes
Fresh peaches
Lemons

3 $\frac{1}{2}$-lb packets of frozen spinach
4 oz Cheddar cheese
$\frac{1}{2}$ pt double cream
1 pt milk

MENU 33 *Summer Family Supper*

Kidneys Richard

Boiled Rice

Crunchy Flapjacks

Kidneys Richard

2 lb veal kidneys
1 lb button mushrooms
3 tablespoons Brandy
3 tablespoons tomato purée

$\frac{1}{2}$ pt single cream
2 oz butter
Salt and pepper

Cut the kidneys into small dice and cover with cold water. Leave to stand for half an hour. Wash the mushrooms and cut into fine slices. Set aside.

Drain and dry the kidneys. Melt the butter in a large shallow pan. Throw in the kidneys. Fry slowly, stirring constantly, until the kidneys start to brown slightly. Add the mushrooms and fry together for another 5 minutes. Warm the Brandy in a separate pan and set it alight, pour over the kidneys, and shake the pan to keep the flames going for as long as possible. Blend the tomato purée with the cream, and as soon as the flames from the Brandy have died away pour the cream over the meat mixture. Stir well and allow to bubble for 2 or 3 minutes.

Season with salt and black pepper and serve at once with a dish of boiled rice (for method see Menu 4, page 14) which has been cooked and kept hot over steam.

Crunchy Flapjacks

3 oz butter
2 oz golden syrup (2 large tablespoons)
2 oz porridge oats
3 oz brown sugar

2 oz nuts coarsely chopped
2 oz cornflakes (most breakfast cereals will do, i.e. Coco Pops or Puffed Wheat)

Gently melt the butter and golden syrup in a large saucepan. Add all the other ingredients. Stir together well. Grease a shallow rectangular tin (a Swiss Roll tin is perfect). Put the mixture into this tin, smoothing it down evenly and pushing it into the corners. Bake at 350° F. or Reg. 4 for 20 minutes. Let it cool in the tin.

Mark into squares with the back of a knife. Allow it to become quite cold. Cut through the marks with a sharp knife and take out of the tin gently. This keeps well in a cake-tin. But if you have children you won't be able to keep it long. I can't.

Shopping List	2 lb veal kidneys	Small tin tomato purée
	1 lb button mushrooms	Porridge oats and Cornflakes
	2 oz nuts	$\frac{1}{2}$ pt single cream
	1 lb Italian rice	Brandy

MENU 34 *Summer Family Supper*

Ham Pastries

Green Salad with Avocado

Strawberries and Cream

Ham Pastries

12 large slices of ham	2 packets frozen puff pastry
1 oz butter	1 egg
1 tablespoon flour	Pepper, nutmeg
$\frac{1}{2}$ pt milk	3 tablespoons water
6 tablespoons Parmesan cheese	

Melt the butter in a saucepan, add the flour, and stir well over a gentle heat for 3 or 4 minutes. Add the milk gradually, stirring all the time. Allow it to cook gently for about 10 minutes stirring occasionally. Season with pepper and nutmeg. Spread each slice of ham with the sauce and sprinkle with half a tablespoon of Parmesan. Roll up neatly. Roll out pastry and cut into 12 squares. Wrap each ham roll in a square of puff pastry. Separate the egg. Beat the white slightly and seal the pastry rolls with egg white. Beat the egg yolk and blend with the water. Glaze each pastry with the egg yolk and water mixture. Set on a greased baking sheet. Preheat the oven to 425° F. or Reg. 7. Bake the pastries for 15 or 20 minutes until they are raised and golden brown. Serve at once.

Green Salad with Avocado

1 large Cos lettuce	French dressing (recipe on
1 avocado pear	page 137)
3 tablespoons chopped parsley	

Wash and dry the lettuce and tear into large chunks. Put into a salad bowl. Peel the avocado and cut into slices. Strew the slices over the lettuce and sprinkle the parsley over the top. Pour the dressing over. Turn gently with 2 spoons and serve at once.

This salad must be prepared at the last moment as the avocado will turn black if allowed to stand.

S.M.—7

Strawberries *and Cream*	2 lb ripe strawberries 4 oz caster sugar	$\frac{1}{2}$ pt double cream

Hull the strawberries, rinse quickly under a cold tap and leave to drain. Turn into a large bowl and sprinkle with the caster sugar. Leave in a cool place (but not in the fridge), for 1 to 2 hours, turning occasionally to distribute the sugar right through the strawberries.

Serve with thick cream separately.

Shopping List

1 Cos lettuce	12 large slices of ham
1 avocado pear	2 packets frozen puff pastry
Parsley	Parmesan cheese
2 lb strawberries	$\frac{1}{2}$ pt double cream

MENU 35 *Summer Family Supper*

Shrimp Fritters

Tomato Salad

Raspberry Meringue Tarts and Whipped Cream

Shrimp Fritters	8 oz flour	1 lb peeled shrimps
	¼ pt milk	Salt, black pepper
	2 eggs	Fat or oil for frying
	1 tablespoon oil	

Put the flour into a fairly large bowl, and make a well in the centre. Drop in the eggs, the oil, and the salt and pepper. Mix together well. Stir in the milk gradually. Beat well until smooth. Stir in the shrimps. Heat the fat or oil in a fairly deep chip pan until hot but not smoking. Drop tablespoonfuls of the mixture into the oil and fry until golden brown.

Drain well and serve very hot, garnished with parsley and lemon quarters.

| *Tomato Salad* | 2 lb tomatoes | 2 tablespoons chopped parsley |
| | 1 small onion | French dressing (recipe on page 137) |

Peel the tomatoes and slice them thickly. Lay on a flat dish. Peel the onion, slice very thinly, and separate the slices into rings. Strew the rings liberally over the tomatoes and sprinkle with 2 or 3 tablespoonfuls of French dressing. Leave in a cold place for 1 hour and sprinkle with chopped parsley at the moment of service.

Raspberry
Meringue
Tarts and
Whipped
Cream

3 egg whites	1 punnet raspberries
11 tablespoons caster sugar	½ pt double cream

Whisk the egg whites until stiff and fold in 7 tablespoons of sugar. Whisk again until thick and shiny, and fold in 4 tablespoons of sugar. Blend well without beating. Brush a baking sheet with vegetable oil. Drop the meringue mixture on to the tin in 12 evenly sized mounds. Hollow out each mound with a teaspoon to make tart shapes. Bake at 200° F. or Reg. 2 for 2 hours until the tarts are firm and a pale biscuit colour.

Fill the centres with raspberries and serve with the cream, whipped, and a separate bowl of caster sugar. If you put the sugar on the raspberries the meringues will go soggy. Fill the tarts at the moment of service and they will be crisp.

Shopping List

1 lb peeled shrimps	1 punnet raspberries
3 lemons	Caster sugar
2 lb tomatoes	6 eggs
Parsley	½ pt double cream

MENU 36 *Summer Family Supper*

Prawn Risotto

Lettuce Salad

Blackcurrant Ice Cream

Prawn Risotto

1 Spanish onion	4 tomatoes
1 lb Italian rice	1 lb peeled prawns (frozen
4 oz butter	will do)
2 tablespoons oil	Salt and pepper
3 pt chicken stock	Parmesan cheese

Melt 2 oz butter and the oil gently in a large shallow pan. Add the onion very finely chopped, and fry slowly until it is clear and pale. Add the rice and fry until the rice is transparent and soaked

in butter and oil. Add just enough hot stock to cover the rice, stir well. Cook gently until the stock is absorbed and then add some more. Carry on like this until all the stock has been absorbed and the rice is tender. Stir frequently to prevent it from sticking and do not allow it to become dry. When you add the last lot of stock stir in the prawns, and tomatoes—peeled, seeded, and chopped. When all the stock has been absorbed stir in the remaining 2 oz butter, season to taste, and serve at once with plenty of grated Parmesan cheese, handed round separately.

The whole operation from start to finish should take 45 minutes if you cook at the correct slow, even temperature.

Lettuce Salad   As for Menu 9, see pages 26 and 11.

Blackcurrant *Ice Cream*	4 egg yolks 1 pt double cream	$\frac{1}{4}$ pt Ribena

Bring the Ribena to the boil. Pour slowly on to the beaten egg yolks, stirring constantly. Then whip until cold. Whisk the cream until it is thick but not too stiff and fold into the egg yolk mixture. Freeze for at least 4 hours. It is not necessary to stir this mixture during freezing owing to the high fat content.

This obviously is not a cheap meal but delicious on a warm summer evening when one is entertaining informally. It goes well with a game of bridge.

Shopping List

1 lb peeled prawns
1 Spanish onion
2 lettuces
4 tomatoes
1 lb Italian rice

2 chicken bouillon cubes
Parmesan cheese
Ribena
1 pt double cream

94

MENU 37 *Summer Family Supper*

Cold Chicken with Chopped Aspic

Rice Salad

French Saucer Pancakes

---

*Cold Chicken
with Chopped
Aspic*

1 large roasting chicken
Salt and pepper
Butter

Lettuce heart
1 packet of aspic powder

Season the chicken inside and out with plenty of salt and pepper. Spread the breast with soft butter. Preheat the oven at 350° F. or Reg. 4. Roast the chicken, basting frequently and turning every 20 minutes until the chicken is golden and tender (about 1 hour). Put on to a plate and allow to become absolutely cold. Make up the aspic powder according to the directions and leave to set firm. Carve the chicken into neat portions and lay on a dish. Surround with chopped aspic and lettuce leaves.

Serve separately with very thick home-made mayonnaise (see recipe on page 138) and rice salad.

Rice Salad

8 oz Italian rice
4 tomatoes
½ cucumber
1 yellow pepper

4 oz black olives
Oil and vinegar
Salt, black pepper, nutmeg

Boil the rice in plenty of salted water until tender; drain and rinse under the cold tap. Shake the sieve to get rid of all the surplus water. Put into a large mixing bowl and season with salt and pepper and grated nutmeg. Stir in 2 tablespoons vinegar and 6 tablespoons oil. Take the seeds out of the tomatoes and cut the flesh into small dice. Add to the rice. Cut the cucumber and the de-seeded pepper into very small dice, add to the rice together with the drained black olives. Mix very well and turn into a salad bowl. Set in the refrigerator for at least 1 hour, preferably longer. This will keep several days in the fridge, if it is covered.

French Saucer Pancakes	3 oz butter	3 oz self-raising flour
	3 eggs	The grated rind of 1 lemon
	3 oz caster sugar	Jam (6 tablespoons)
	¾ pt milk	

Grease 12 saucers with butter. Cream butter, sugar, and lemon rind together until light and pale. Beat in the eggs one by one, and fold in the flour thoroughly. Add the milk gradually, beating until smooth. Divide between the saucers putting the same amount into each one. Bake at 400° F. or Reg. 6 for 15 minutes.

Heat the jam gently until just hot but not boiling. Sandwich the pancakes together in pairs with a tablespoon of warm jam and serve at once sprinkled with more caster sugar.

Shopping List	1 large roasting chicken	Black olives
	1 lettuce	1 packet aspic powder
	½ lb tomatoes	Italian rice
	½ cucumber	1 lb jam
	1 yellow pepper	1 pt milk
	1 lemon	

MENU 38 *Summer Family Supper*

Ostende Tomatoes

Apple Cake

Ostende Tomatoes

12 large tomatoes
12 oz shelled prawns
1 head celery

½ pt thick home-made mayonnaise (recipe on page 138)

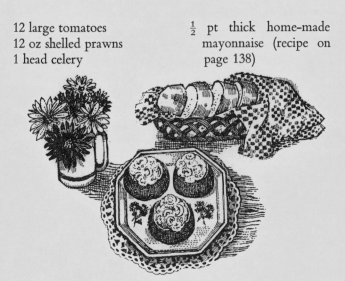

Cut a thin slice off the stem end of each tomato, empty out all the seeds and pulp, and turn them upside down on a grid. Leave to drain for half an hour. Clean the celery and chop very finely. Mix together the prawns, celery, and mayonnaise. Pile into the tomato cases and serve fairly promptly with hot, French bread.

You need very large tomatoes for this; the French ones that are obtainable in Soho during the summer months are the best as they are very big and have an intense flavour. This may not sound very filling but, in fact, it is.

Apple Cake

6 oz flour
6 oz sugar
2 teaspoons baking powder
1 lightly beaten egg
3 oz butter, melted

4 oz sultanas
4 oz chopped nuts (any kind will do but Brazil nuts are best)
2 large cooking apples (peeled, cored, and diced)

Mix everything together, it does not matter in what order. I just put everything into a large bowl as I measure it. Blend it together very well with a large metal spoon. Grease a square or oblong cake tin. Turn the mixture into it and bake at 400° F. or Reg. 6 for 40 minutes or until the apple is tender (prod it with a fork).

Turn it out on to a dish and serve hot or warm—with cream if you like.

Shopping List   12 oz shelled prawns   4 oz peeled nuts
                   12 very large tomatoes   Sultanas
                   1 head celery   French bread
                   2 large cooking apples

MENU 39 *Summer Family Supper*

Ham and Cheese Tart

Lettuce Salad

Baked Peaches

Ham and
Cheese Tart

$\frac{1}{4}$ lb ham	$\frac{1}{2}$ lb shortcrust pastry
3 eggs	$\frac{1}{2}$ pt milk
2 oz grated Cheddar cheese	Black pepper, nutmeg

Line a flan tin with shortcrust pastry. Chop the ham and scatter over the pastry base. Strew the grated cheese over the ham. Beat the eggs with a good scrape of black pepper and nutmeg. Add the milk and whisk again. Pour the egg and milk mixture over the ham and cheese.

Preheat the oven to 400° F. or Reg. 6. Bake the flan at this temperature for 5 minutes then reduce the heat to 310° F. or Reg. 2, and bake for about 20 minutes until the filling is firm. Leave to stand in a warm place, not the oven, for 10 minutes before cutting.

Lettuce Salad   As for Menu 9, see pages 26 and 11.

Baked Peaches

6 large yellow peaches	1 lemon
6 tablespoons brown sugar	1 oz butter

Peel the peaches and cut into halves. Lay cut side down on a large fireproof dish. Squeeze the lemon and sprinkle the juice over the peaches. Strew over the sugar. Divide the butter into small pieces and dot over the top. Bake at 310° F. or Reg. 2 for 20 minutes, basting occasionally. Serve very hot.

This is delicious alone but even nicer served with vanilla ice cream.

Shopping List
2 lettuces	$\frac{1}{4}$ lb ham
6 large yellow peaches	$\frac{1}{2}$ lb shortcrust pastry
1 lemon	Cheddar cheese

MENU 40 *Summer Family Supper*

Smoked Haddock Soufflés

Pêche Cœur à la Crème

Smoked Haddock Soufflés

1 lb smoked haddock fillets	2 tablespoons flour
1 pt milk	2 oz butter
4 eggs	Salt and pepper

Simmer the haddock in the milk until it is cooked, strain the fish (reserving the milk), take the skin off and mash with a fork until fairly smooth. Melt the butter and stir in the flour. Add the milk

slowly and beat until smooth. Bring to the boil and simmer for 5 minutes. Cool. Separate the eggs and beat the yolks into the milk mixture one by one. Stir in the fish and season with salt and pepper. Whisk the egg whites until stiff but not dry. Fold into the egg yolk mixture. Pour into 12 buttered individual soufflé dishes, filling the dishes half full. Bake at 350° F. or Reg. 4 for 20 minutes. Serve *at once*.

This is lovely with hot crisp toast.

Pêche Cœur $\frac{1}{2}$ oz gelatine $\frac{3}{4}$ lb cream cheese
à la Crème $\frac{1}{4}$ pt single cream   Small tin peaches

Strain the peaches, reserving the juice, and purée or sieve them until smooth. Take 3 tablespoons of the peach juice and add the gelatine. Heat gently until the gelatine has dissolved. Add to the peach purée. Beat the cream cheese and cream together until smooth. Blend the two mixtures together thoroughly. Take a heart-shaped cake tin and brush lightly with oil. Pour in the mixture and refrigerate until set. Obviously the heart-shaped mould is not really necessary, but it looks pretty.

Shopping List 1 lb smoked haddock fillets $\frac{3}{4}$ lb cream cheese
                 Gelatine $\frac{1}{4}$ pt single cream
                 Small tin peaches   1 pt milk

102

MENU 41 *Summer Family Supper*

Raçitura

Treacle Tart

Raçitura This is a Romanian dish. It may sound revolting and outlandish, but in fact it is neither; it is rather like good home-made brawn.

4 lb pigs' trotters	3 bay leaves
1 Spanish onion	A little salt
1 large carrot	1 Cos lettuce
1 garlic clove	Home-made mayonnaise
Black peppercorns	

Wash the pigs' trotters thoroughly and singe off any hairs. Put into a large deep saucepan. Add the onion, carrot, garlic, and seasonings. Cover with cold water. Bring to the boil slowly taking off all the scum as it rises. Cover and cook slowly for half an hour. Take the lid off and cook very slowly for a further 2 hours. Strain off the liquor and set aside, discarding the vegetables. Cool the trotters and take out all the bones (this is a messy job). Cut all the meat into cubes. Put into a deep pudding basin, cover, and leave both the meat and the bowl of stock in the fridge overnight. The next day take the bowl of stock which should have set to a solid jelly and take off every scrap of fat. Heat the stock gently until it just melts. Cool again until syrupy and pour over the meat, filling the bowl to the brim. Refrigerate again until set solid.

Cut the Cos lettuce into large chunks and cover the base of round dish. Turn out the mould in the centre and serve with a sauceboat full of thick home-made mayonnaise (recipe on page 138).

103

Treacle Tart ½ lb shortcrust pastry   1 lemon
3 oz soft white breadcrumbs   ½ lb golden syrup

Line a flan tin with pastry. Strew over the breadcrumbs. Squeeze
the juice from the lemon, add to the syrup, and then pour over the
breadcrumbs. Bake at 350° F. or Reg. 4 for about 20 minutes until
the filling is brown and set. Allow to become cold but do not
refrigerate it.

Shopping List   4 lb pigs' trotters   1 lemon
1 Spanish onion   ½ lb shortcrust pastry
1 large carrot   1 tin golden syrup
1 Cos lettuce   1 small stale loaf

WINTER
LUNCHEONS
AND FAMILY
SUPPERS

MENU 42 *Winter Luncheon*

Hors d'Œuvre: Carrot Salad

Sardines

Radishes

Chicken with Herbs

Steamed Potatoes, Lettuce Salad

Crispy Apple Flan

Hors
d'Œuvre:
Carrot Salad

As for Menu 21, see page 55.

Sardines

2 large tins sardines   Oil   Lemons

Drain the oil from the sardines. Put into the dish. Sprinkle with oil and garnish with lemon quarters.

Radishes

As for Menu 26, see page 67.

Chicken
with Herbs

2 medium chickens or 1 capon	3 oz butter
2 tablespoons chopped parsley	$\frac{1}{4}$ pt single cream
2 tablespoons chopped tarragon	2 tablespoons white wine
1 tablespoon chopped rosemary	Salt and pepper
2 large tomatoes	

Mash up 2 oz butter with salt, pepper, and the herbs, and mix with the tomatoes cut into eighths. Stuff the chickens with this mixture. Spread the chickens with the rest of the butter and season. Roast at 400° F. or Reg. 6 for 45 minutes until brown and tender for smaller chickens, or 1½ hours for a large one. Carve the chickens into portions and put on to a serving dish. Put the wine into the roasting tin, give a good stir round and bring to the boil. Cook for 2 minutes and add the cream. Heat through and strain over the chicken. This will keep warm while you eat your first course.

Steamed Potatoes   As for Menu 19, see page 51.

Lettuce Salad   As for Menu 9, see pages 26 and 11.

Crispy Apple Flan   6 oz cornflakes   1½ lb cooking apples
6 oz butter   3 oz brown sugar

Crush the cornflakes into crumbs with a rolling pin. Melt 4 oz butter and mix with the cornflake crumbs. Put into a large shallow fireproof dish. Press well down. Bake for 10 minutes at 335° F. or Reg. 3. Cool. Peel and core the apples and cut into thick slices. Melt the remaining butter and fry the apples gently for 2 to 3 minutes. Sprinkle with 2 oz brown sugar and cook gently until the sugar starts to melt and caramelize (see Glossary, page 140). Put the whole panful into the cornflake case and sprinkle with the rest of the sugar. Put back into the oven until the sugar on the top starts to melt and caramelize. Serve cold or warm with cream.

Shopping List

2 medium chickens	1½ lb cooking apples
1 lb carrots	Tarragon
2 bunches radishes	Rosemary
2 lemons	2 large tins sardines
Parsley	Cornflakes
½ lb tomatoes	½ lb butter
2 lb potatoes	¼ pt single cream
2 lettuces	White wine

Hors d'Œuvre: Cucumber Salad

Celeriac Remoulade

Salami with Black Olives

Fillet of Beef with Tomato Fondue

Jacket Potatoes

Orange Salad with Cointreau

Hors d'Œuvre: Cucumber Salad

1 cucumber
Chopped parsley

French dressing (recipe on page 137)

Peel the cucumber and cut off the top and bottom. Cut in half lengthways. Take a teaspoon and run firmly down the cut halves of the cucumber lifting out all the seeds. Scrape them all away and cut the cucumber into thick slices. Put into a shallow dish and sprinkle with French dressing and chopped parsley.

Celeriac Remoulade

1 head of celeriac

$\frac{1}{4}$ pt home-made mayonnaise (recipe on page 138)

Peel the celeriac and shred finely on a mandoline slicer (see Glossary, page 140). Rinse in acidulated water (water to which a dash of vinegar has been added) and drain well. Mix with the mayonnaise, and serve on a flat dish.

Salami with Black Olives

$\frac{3}{4}$ lb Italian salami cut very thin

$\frac{1}{4}$ lb black olives

Arrange the salami neatly on a flat dish leaving a space in the centre. Pile the olives in a little mound in the middle.

Fillet of Beef with Tomato Fondue	2½ lb fillet of beef rolled with flare fat and tied	1 tablespoon Brandy
		1 tablespoon Madeira
	2 oz butter	1 tablespoon chopped parsley
	1 Spanish onion	2 tablespoons water
	1 medium tin tomatoes	Salt, pepper, and nutmeg

Rub the beef with salt and pepper and spread with ½ oz butter. Roast at 400° F. or Reg. 6 for 45 minutes. Leave to stand in a warm place 10–15 minutes before carving. Carve into thick slices and serve with the fondue.

TOMATO FONDUE

Melt the remaining butter and cook the finely sliced onion in it until very soft but not browned. Add the tomatoes and cook slowly until it is thick. Add salt and pepper, Brandy and Madeira and a good scrape of nutmeg. Pour the fat off the roasting tin and add the water to it. Bring to the boil, stirring round the dish to dissolve all the essence from the meat. Add this to the sauce and boil fairly hard for 2 or 3 minutes, then stir in the chopped parsley and serve.

Jacket Potatoes   As for Menu 16, see page 43.

Orange Salad with Cointreau	8 oranges	3 tablespoons caster sugar
	3 tablespoons Cointreau	

Peel the oranges and cut into very thin slices. Arrange in neat circles on a fairly flat dish. Sprinkle with caster sugar and Cointreau. Allow to stand in a cool place (not the refrigerator) for 2 hours.

Shopping List	2½ lb fillet of beef	1 medium tin tomatoes
	1 Spanish onion	¾ lb Italian salami
	1 cucumber	¼ lb black olives
	Parsley	1 miniature bottle Cointreau
	1 head celeriac	Brandy
	6 large potatoes	Madeira
	8 oranges	

MENU 44 *Winter Luncheon*

Salade Niçoise

Veal Maison

Pommes Purées

Petits Pois

Crème Caramel

Salade Niçoise

1 lettuce
3 tomatoes
1 green pepper
3 sticks celery
Small tin tunny fish

Small tin anchovies in oil
3 hard-boiled eggs
2 oz black olives
French dressing (recipe on page 137)

Wash the lettuce and dry it. Cut the tomatoes and eggs into quarters. Cut the celery and anchovies into small pieces. Drain and flake the tunny fish. Core and de-seed the pepper and cut into thin rings. Arrange all the ingredients in a bowl. Pour the dressing over at the moment of service and mix at the table.

Serve with hot French bread.

Veal Maison

2½ lb pie-veal
1 Spanish onion
2 oz butter
½ lb baby onions
½ lb button mushrooms

1 tablespoon flour
1 teacup white wine
¼ pt single cream
Salt and pepper

Cut the veal into small dice. Chop the Spanish onion very finely. Melt the butter in a pan, add the onion and cook until golden. Add the meat and fry until it starts to brown, sprinkle with flour and cook for 2 minutes, stirring constantly. Pour over the white wine. Bring to the boil. Put into a casserole. Cover and put in a slow oven at 335° F. or Reg. 3 for 2 hours. After 1 hour add the peeled baby onions. After 1½ hours add the quartered mushrooms. Stir in the cream and serve. This can be made in advance up to the point where you add the cream and reheated when required.

Pommes Purées   As for Menu 2, see page 7.

Petits Pois   2 medium tins French petits pois   1 oz butter

Drain the liquid off of the peas. Melt the butter in a saucepan. Heat the peas gently with the butter until they are hot through.

Crème Caramel   1 pt milk   6 oz vanilla sugar (recipe on page 139)
    2 tablespoons water   4 eggs

Heat 2 oz sugar and 2 tablespoons water in a saucepan, stirring until the sugar is dissolved. Bring to the boil and cook rapidly until the caramel is a deep rich brown (be careful not to burn it!). Pour the caramel into a deep fireproof dish, and tilt the dish in all directions until it is coated with the caramel. Beat the eggs and remaining sugar together until thick. Bring the milk to the boil and pour on to the eggs. Beat well. Strain the egg and milk mixture into the fireproof dish. Set the dish into a tin containing 1 inch of water.

Bake at 300° F. or Reg. 2 for 1 hour or until a knife plunged into the centre comes out clean.

Leave until ice-cold and turn out just before serving. Do not use a flat dish because the juices will overflow if you do.

Shopping List

2½ lb pie-veal
½ lb baby onions
½ lb button mushrooms
1 lettuce
½ lb tomatoes
1 green pepper
1 head celery
1 Spanish onion
2 lb potatoes

1 small tin anchovies in oil
2 oz black olives
1 small tin tunny fish
2 medium tins petits pois
6 eggs
¼ pt single cream
1 pt milk
French bread
White wine

Hors d'Œuvre: Salade Creole

Coppa

Calves Liver with Courgettes

Crusty Potato Bake

Chocolate Fudge Pudding

Hors
d'Œuvre:
Salade Creole

1 lb tomatoes	½ Spanish onion
2 green peppers	French dressing (recipe on page 137)

Skin the tomatoes and cut them into quarters. Put into a bowl. Core and de-seed the peppers and cut into thin rings. Cut the onion into the thinnest possible slices. Separate into rings. Strew the pepper and onion rings over the tomatoes. Pour over the dressing and leave to marinate for 1 hour.

Coppa This is a raw smoked ham sausage obtainable at good Italian delicatessen shops. Have it cut in the thinnest possible slices. For 6 people you will need about half a pound.

Calves Liver
with
Courgettes

1½ lb calves liver cut into very thin slices	1 medium tin tomatoes
2 Spanish onions	3 tablespoons oil
2 cloves garlic	Salt and pepper
½ lb courgettes	½ pt milk

Cut the liver into squares, put in bowl and cover with the milk. Soak for 15 minutes.

Heat the oil gently in a large sauté pan. Slice the onions and chop the garlic. Fry the onions and garlic gently for 5 minutes. Drain and dry the liver and add to the pan. Fry the liver gently, stirring constantly, until it is light brown. Slice the unpeeled courgettes very thin and add to the pan together with the tomatoes and seasoning. Stir until well mixed. Cover the pan and simmer very gently for 10 minutes. Serve at once.

Crusty Potato Bake

| 3 lb potatoes | 3 oz beef or chicken |
| Salt and pepper | dripping |

Peel the potatoes and cook in salted water until tender. Drain well and mash until absolutely free from lumps. Grease a deep fireproof dish with ½ oz dripping. Beat 2 oz dripping into the potatoes until well blended. Season it. Put the potato mixture into the fireproof dish. Dot with the remaining dripping. Bake at 335° F. or Reg. 3 for 2 hours. This should be crisp and golden on the top and crusty round the sides of the dish.

Chocolate Fudge Pudding

4 oz flour	2 oz butter
1 teaspoon baking powder	1 oz glacé cherries
4 oz caster sugar	2 oz brown sugar
2 oz powdered drinking chocolate	¾ pt boiling water
¼ pt milk	

Mix together flour, baking powder, caster sugar, and 1 oz chocolate. Melt the butter. Add the melted butter and milk to the dry ingredients, and beat until smooth. Cut the cherries into pieces and add. Pour the mixture into a fireproof dish. Pour over the boiling water. Stand for 5 minutes. Mix the remaining 1 oz chocolate and the brown sugar together, and strew on top of the mixture. Bake at 335° F. or Reg. 3 for 1 hour. Serve hot.

Shopping List

1½ lb calves liver	3 lb potatoes
1 lb tomatoes	½ lb coppa
2 green peppers	1 medium tin tomatoes
3 Spanish onions	1 oz glacé cherries
½ lb courgettes	1 pt milk

MENU 46 *Winter Luncheon*

Buttered Shrimps

Pork Chops

Peppers au Gratin

Gâteau de Riz

| *Buttered* | 12 oz shrimps | Black pepper |
| *Shrimps* | 6 oz butter | |

Divide the shrimps into 6 fireproof ramekins. Put 1 oz butter on each dish. Season each one with a twist of black pepper from a pepper mill. Put into a medium oven, 400° F. or Reg. 6, for 10 minutes until the butter is melted and the shrimps are very hot. Do not leave in the oven a moment longer as the shrimps will become tough. Serve at once with hot rolls or *croissants* and very cold butter.

| *Pork Chops* | 6 pork chops cut with the kidney | Salt and pepper |
| | Small knob of dripping | |

Melt the dripping in a frying pan. Fry the chops until they are light brown on each side. Drain them and lay them in a roasting tin. Season them. Put into a medium oven, 400° F. or Reg. 6, for half an hour, turning them over at half time. These will keep warm on a serving dish while you eat your first course.

Peppers	1 lb tomatoes	3 tablespoons breadcrumbs
au Gratin	3 green peppers	3 tablespoons grated
	2 Spanish onions	Cheddar cheese
	2 oz butter	Salt and pepper

115

Put the peppers under a hot grill, turning them round and round until they are black. The skins will then slip off easily. Take out the cores and seeds from the skinned peppers and cut them into thin slices. Skin and slice the tomatoes. Butter a shallow baking dish and put in the sliced tomatoes. Peel and slice the onions and fry them in butter until golden. Drain well and put on top of the tomatoes. Lay the peppers on top of the onions. Season with salt and black pepper. Mix the breadcrumbs and grated cheese together and strew over the peppers. Sprinkle with the butter remaining in the frying pan. Bake at 400° F. or Reg. 6 for three-quarters of an hour.

Gâteau de Riz

4 oz Italian rice	4 oz butter
1 pt milk	3 oz sugar
4 eggs	2 teaspoons almond extract

Cook the rice in the milk for 15 minutes. Cool. Cream the butter and sugar until pale. Add the egg yolks one by one, beating well in between each addition. Stir in the almond extract and the rice and milk. Whisk the egg whites until stiff. Fold the whites into the rice mixture. Pour into a shallow buttered pie dish and bake at 335° F. or Reg. 3 for 1 hour. Serve cold.

Shopping List

6 pork chops	Almond extract
12 oz shrimps	$\frac{1}{2}$ lb butter
1 lb tomatoes	1 pt milk
3 green peppers	Cheddar cheese
2 Spanish onions	Rolls or *croissants*
Italian rice	

Tunny Fish and Tomato Salad

Racks of Lamb

Roast Potatoes, Braised Chicory

Apricot Fool

Tunny Fish   2 large tins tunny fish   2 tablespoons chopped parsley
and Tomato   1 lb tomatoes   French dressing (recipe on
Salad   ½ Spanish onion   page 137)

Slice the tomatoes thinly and arrange in overlapping circles on a flat dish. Drain and flake the tunny fish. Pile in the centre of the tomatoes. Slice the half onion thinly and separate the slices into rings. Scatter the rings over the dish. Pour over 4 tablespoons French dressing and sprinkle with chopped parsley. Leave to stand for about an hour.

Racks of Lamb   2 loins of lamb, chined   Salt and pepper
               2 oz soft butter

Ask the butcher to chine (i.e. to chop out the backbone, making it easy to carve) the loins of lamb and trim the surplus fat from the joints. Salt and pepper them and spread with soft butter. Pre-heat the oven to 400° F. or Reg. 6. Roast the joints, basting frequently for about an hour. Allow to rest for 15 minutes in a warm oven before carving.

Roast Potatoes   2½ lb potatoes   Salt

Peel and quarter the potatoes. Put them into cold salted water. Bring to the boil and cook slowly for 10 minutes. Drain well. Put

117

into the roasting tin round the meat as soon as the fat has started to run. Turn the potatoes over at least once during the cooking time.

| *Braised Chicory* | 2 lb chicory
2 oz butter | 1 lemon
Salt and pepper |

Wipe the chicory with a clean cloth. Cut off the stalk ends and trim off any leaves that look brown or discoloured. Cut into halves lengthways. Lay in a fireproof dish. Put in the butter cut into pieces, the juice of the lemon, and salt and pepper. Cover the dish and cook in the oven at 400° F. or Reg. 6 for 40 minutes.

| *Apricot Fool* | 12 oz dried apricots
3 oz vanilla sugar (recipe on
page 139) | $\frac{1}{2}$ pt water
$\frac{1}{2}$ pt double cream |

Cook the apricots, sugar, and water together gently until the apricots are very soft. Put the whole contents of the saucepan through a sieve or purée in a blender. It should be a thick smooth purée. Whip the cream lightly until thickened, but not stiff. Blend the cream and apricot purée well together. Refrigerate the mixture in a serving bowl until very cold, for at least 2 hours.

Shopping List

2 loins of lamb (chined)   2 lb chicory
1 lb tomatoes $\frac{3}{4}$ lb dried apricots
1 lemon   2 large tins tunny fish
1 Spanish onion $\frac{1}{2}$ lb butter
Parsley $\frac{1}{2}$ pt double cream
$2\frac{1}{2}$ lb potatoes

MENU 48 *Winter Family Supper*

Salmon Pudding

Cucumber Salad

Baked Apples

Salmon   2 oz butter   ½ head celery
Pudding 3 tablespoons flour   1 onion
            ¾ pt milk   4 eggs
            Salt and pepper   2 tablespoons chopped parsley
            2 large tins of salmon

Make a white sauce with the butter, flour, and milk (recipe on page 139). Drain and flake the salmon. Add to the sauce with the onion and celery, both minced. Separate the eggs. Whisk the whites until stiff. Stir the egg yolks and parsley into the salmon mixture. Season with salt and pepper. Fold in the egg whites. Pour into a greased fireproof dish and bake at 350° F. or Reg. 4 for 40 minutes. Serve at once.

Cucumber   As for Menu 6, see page 19.
Salad

Baked Apples   6 large cooking apples   6 tablespoons water
              6 teaspoons sultanas   1 teaspoon powdered cinnamon
              6 tablespoons Demerara sugar

Core the apples and cut a strip of peel right round the centres of the apples. Put the water and the apples into a fireproof dish. Put one teaspoon sultanas into the centre of each apple. Mix the sugar and cinnamon together, and put a tablespoonful into each apple. Bake at 350° F. or Reg. 4 for 40 minutes, basting occasionally.

Serve hot with thick cream.

Shopping List

1 head celery
Parsley
1 onion
1 cucumber
6 cooking apples

2 large tins of salmon
Sultanas
½ pt thick cream
1 pt milk

MENU 49 *Winter Family Supper*

Ham Pancakes

Chicory and Beetroot Salad

Baked Bananas with Rum

Ham Pancakes

6 large *thin* slices of ham (or 12 smaller ones)
6 heaped tablespoons flour
3 oz butter
2 eggs

3 oz grated Gruyère cheese
$\frac{1}{2}$ pt single cream
Milk
Black pepper
Lard

Make a pancake batter with flour, eggs, 1 oz melted butter, and enough milk to make a batter of the consistency of thin cream (blend together flour, eggs, and butter smoothly, then add milk as needed). Make 12 thin pancakes using the lard to lubricate the pan. Butter well a shallow fireproof dish with $\frac{1}{2}$ oz butter. Lay half a slice of ham on each pancake (or a whole slice if they are small). Roll up each pancake and lay side by side in the fireproof dish. Season with black pepper. Strew the grated Gruyère cheese over the pancakes. Pour over the thin cream. Dot with the last $1\frac{1}{2}$ oz butter. Bake at 350° F. or Reg. 4 for 20 minutes.

Chicory and Beetroot Salad

As for Menu 2, see page 7.

Baked Bananas with Rum

6 large bananas
6 tablespoons Rum

1 oz butter
6 tablespoons Demerara sugar

Peel the bananas, lay them side by side in a fireproof dish. Pour over the Rum, sprinkle with Demerara sugar, and dot with the butter. Bake at 350° F. or Reg. 4 for half an hour, turning the bananas over at half time. Serve very hot.

121

Shopping List

1 lb chicory
1 lb beetroot
6 bananas
6 large thin slices of ham

Gruyère cheese
½ pt single cream
Rum

MENU 50 *Winter Family Supper*

Hash with Eggs

Cherry Almond Pudding

Hash with Eggs

6 potatoes
1 Spanish onion
3 slices of ham
3 slices of tinned tongue

2 oz good dripping
6 eggs
Salt and pepper

Peel the potatoes and cook them gently in boiling salted water until they are just tender. Drain and allow to become cold. Cut into very small dice. Chop the onion finely. Melt the dripping in a saucepan, add the onion and cook gently until soft but not browned. Add the potato, fry gently, stirring occasionally, until pale gold. Chop the ham and tongue and add to the potatoes. Season with salt and pepper. Mix well together. Turn the mixture into a large shallow fireproof dish. Make six indentations with the back of a tablespoon. Drop an egg into each hollow. Bake at 350° F. or Reg. 4 for 10 minutes until the whites of the eggs are set and the yolks still soft.

Cherry Almond Pudding

1 large tin of cherries
6 oz butter
3 eggs
6 oz caster sugar

6 oz self-raising flour
2 teaspoons almond essence
3 oz slivered blanched almonds

Drain the juice from the cherries and butter a fireproof dish. Put in the cherries. Cream the butter and sugar until fluffy and pale. Beat in the eggs one by one, beating well after each addition. Stir in the flour and almond essence. Pour over the cherries. Strew the slivered, blanched almonds over the top. Bake at 350° F. or Reg. 4 for 45 minutes or until well risen and brown. This is delicious warm or cold.

123

Shopping List

6 medium potatoes
1 Spanish onion
3 slices of ham
3 slices of tinned tongue
1 large tin of cherries

Almond essence
3 oz almonds
6 eggs
½ lb butter

Moussaka

Orange Salad with Almonds

Moussaka

2 lb minced beef
2 Spanish onions
2 aubergines
2 tablespoons oil
1 lb potatoes
2 oz butter

2 tablespoons flour
$\frac{1}{4}$ pt milk
4 oz grated Cheddar cheese
Salt and pepper
2 bay leaves

Boil the potatoes until just tender; cool and cut into thin slices. Peel and slice the onions and fry in 1 tablespoon of oil until transparent; add the beef, seasoning, and bay leaves and fry gently, stirring occasionally, for 20 minutes. Top and tail the aubergines but do not peel. Cut into thin slices lengthways and fry gently on both sides in the remaining tablespoon of oil. Layer the meat and onion mixture and the aubergines in a baking tin or casserole. Arrange the sliced potatoes on the top. Make a cheese sauce with the butter, flour, milk, and cheese. Pour the sauce over the potatoes

and bake at 400° F. or Reg. 6 for half an hour. This can be made the day before or early in the day up to the point where you pour over the cheese sauce.

| *Orange Salad* | 6 seedless oranges | 2 oz flaked almonds |
| *with Almonds* | 3 tablespoons caster sugar | |

Peel the oranges taking off every scrap of white pith. Slice thinly and arrange in overlapping circles on a flat dish. Sprinkle with the caster sugar and strew the flaked almonds over the top.

Serve very cold, with thick fresh cream if you like.

This is very refreshing and light after a rather rich, spicy dish.

Shopping List	2 lb minced beef	6 seedless oranges
	1 lb potatoes	2 oz flaked almonds
	2 Spanish onions	4 oz Cheddar cheese
	2 aubergines	

Creamed Prawns with Rice

Cheese Board with Celery

Creamed Prawns with Rice

1 lb peeled prawns (frozen are all right as long as you defrost them completely)
1 lb Italian rice

4 oz butter
1 large glass of Brandy
$\frac{3}{4}$ pt thick cream
3 tablespoons chopped parsley

Cook the rice in a large amount of salted, boiling water for 12 minutes. Drain and rinse in a metal colander and set over a pan of water. Cover the colander and steam gently while you prepare the prawns.

Melt the butter in a sauté pan and add the prawns. Warm the Brandy in a separate pan, set light to it, and pour it over the prawns. Shake the pan to keep the flames going for as long as possible. After the flames go out simmer for another 2 minutes. Pour the cream over and allow to bubble until the cream thickens. Stir well.

Arrange the rice in a flattened mound on a flat dish, pour the prawn and cream mixture over it and sprinkle with chopped

parsley. Serve at once. This takes less time to cook than it does to write. It is rich and delicious but rather expensive. Never mind. Serve it on pay day.

Cheese Board Serve a good selection of cheese, preferably one soft (Bel Paese or *with Celery* Port Salut type); one blue (Roquefort or Gorgonzola); one hard (Cheddar or Caerphilly), with a big jar of well-scrubbed celery and lots of good biscuits and unsalted butter.

Shopping List

1 lb peeled prawns
Parsley
Celery
1 lb Italian rice

Cheeses
$\frac{3}{4}$ pt double cream
Brandy

Rice Pizza

Orange and Kirsch Soufflés

Rice Pizza

3 large onions
Large tin tomatoes
½ lb mushrooms
2 cloves garlic
4 oz butter

1 lb Italian rice
3 tablespoons chopped parsley
Grated Parmesan cheese
Salt and pepper

Boil the rice in salted water until just tender. Drain and rinse, and leave to drain.

Melt 2 oz butter in a large frying pan; add the onions and garlic, finely chopped. Fry gently until clear and soft. Slice the mushrooms and add to the onions. Add the tomatoes and season. Cook gently until the mixture is thick.

Melt the remaining butter in a large flameproof dish; add the rice and parsley. Heat, stirring constantly, until it is very hot. Pour over the vegetable mixture and serve at once with a bowl of grated Parmesan cheese.

*Orange and
Kirsch
Soufflés*

½ pt fresh orange juice
3 eggs
8 tablespoons caster sugar

½ oz gelatine
3 tablespoons Kirsch
¼ pt whipped cream

Melt the gelatine with the orange juice. Cool. Whisk the egg yolks and sugar until thick and pale. Add the orange juice and gelatine mixture, and the Kirsch, slowly stirring all the time. Whisk the egg whites until very stiff; fold them into the orange juice mixture. Pour into individual soufflé dishes and leave in a cold place to set.

Just before serving put a large dollop of whipped cream on top of each soufflé.

Shopping List

3 Spanish onions
½ lb mushrooms
Parsley
4 oranges
1 large tin tomatoes

1 lb Italian rice
Parmesan cheese
Gelatine
¼ pt double cream
1 miniature bottle of Kirsch

MENU 54 *Winter Family Supper*

Spanish Potato Omelette

Camembert Cheese and Pears

Spanish Potato Omelette You will have to make two omelettes for 6 people but as they are eaten cold this does not matter. Although this does not sound much, it is extremely good and very filling.

4 large potatoes	4 tablespoons oil
2 Spanish onions	Salt and pepper
6 eggs	Chopped parsley

Boil the potatoes until just tender, drain and cool. Cut into quarters lengthways, then into the thinnest possible slices. Beat the eggs well and add salt and pepper.

Chop the onions finely. Heat half the oil in a heavy frying pan. Cook half the onions very slowly in the oil until they start to soften. Add half the potatoes and cook, stirring occasionally, until it is a homogeneous golden mass. Pour over half the eggs, stir well, and cook slowly until the underneath is thoroughly set. Turn over on to a plate and slide back into the pan so that the other side can also cook slowly. When it is cooked through turn on to a dish and sprinkle with chopped parsley. Repeat the whole operation with the other half of the ingredients. When both omelettes are quite cold cut each one into three equal portions.

Serve with a crisp green salad, and hot rolls or French bread with lots of butter.

Camembert Cheese and Pears

1 ripe Camembert	6 ripe pears
2 oz butter	Juice of $\frac{1}{2}$ lemon

Scrape all the skin from a ripe Camembert cheese. Cream the butter until soft, add the cheese, and blend well together. Shape back into the original flat round shape and put in the centre of a flat dish and refrigerate for one hour. Peel the pears leaving them whole and dip each one in lemon juice to stop them discolouring. Set in a ring on the dish round the camembert. Serve very cold.

This may sound revolting but it is in fact delicious and makes a lovely and unusual dessert without much trouble.

Shopping List

4 large potatoes	1 lemon
2 Spanish onions	1 ripe Camembert cheese
Parsley	6 eggs
2 lettuces	French bread or rolls
6 ripe pears	

Creamed Ham and Chicory

Apple Crumble

Creamed Ham and Chicory

3 lb chicory
1 lemon
1 lb lean chopped ham

½ pt single cream
Salt, black pepper
Butter

Wipe the chicory with a clean cloth; cut off the stalk ends and any outside leaves that are discoloured. Cut lengthways into quarters. Take a large flameproof dish or frying pan and butter it well. Lay the chicory in the pan, salt lightly, pepper fairly well, and sprinkle with lemon juice. Dot with more butter. Fry gently over a very low heat for about 15 minutes, turning frequently until the chicory is just tender. Add the chopped ham and mix well in. Pour over the cream and cook until the cream starts to thicken slightly.

Serve at once with lots of hot French bread.

Apple Crumble

6 large cooking apples
10 oz sugar
12 oz flour

8 oz butter
¾ pt water

Butter a large fireproof dish. Put in the water. Peel, core, and slic
the apples. Put into the dish in layers with 5 oz of the sugar. Sif
the flour with the other 5 oz of sugar and rub in the butter unti
the mixture is like coarse breadcrumbs. Pour the mixture over th
apples and bake at 350° F. or Reg. 4 for 1 hour.

Shopping List

3 lb chicory	1 lb caster sugar
1 lemon	$\frac{1}{2}$ lb butter
6 large cooking apples	$\frac{1}{2}$ pt single cream
1 lb lean ham	French bread
1 lb self-raising flour	

Exotic Meatballs

Creamed Potatoes

Banana Fritters

Exotic
Meatballs

2 lb minced beef
4 slices white bread
2 tablespoons Madeira
1 onion
2 teaspoons dried tarragon

4 oz liver pâté
Pepper and salt
Corn meal
Oil

SAUCE

1 onion
1 green pepper
2 cloves garlic
1 medium tin tomatoes
½ pt milk

3 tablespoons cornflour
2 oz butter
1 teaspoon sweet basil
Salt and pepper

Cut up the bread very small. Cover with water and leave to stand. Mince the onion and add to the meat with the chopped tarragon and salt and pepper. Add the pâté and the Madeira. Squeeze the bread dry and add it to the other ingredients. Mix all together thoroughly. Shape into small balls about one inch in diameter. Roll in corn meal and fry in hot oil until brown. Drain well and put into a deep fireproof dish. Cover with the sauce. Heat gently in a medium oven 350° F. or Reg. 4 for half an hour.

Serve with creamed potatoes.

SAUCE

Mince the onion, de-seeded green pepper, and garlic together. Melt the butter in a saucepan, add the vegetables, and cook gently until soft and pale gold. Add the tomatoes, the salt and pepper, and the sweet basil. Cook uncovered for 5 minutes. Blend the cornflour with the milk, add to the other ingredients, bring to the boil and simmer, stirring constantly, until thick. Pour over the meatballs.

This dish can be made ahead of time and reheated when required.

Banana
Fritters

12 bananas
1 egg
4 oz floor
1 tablespoon oil

Light ale
Icing sugar
Fat for frying

Sift the flour into a basin. Add the egg and the oil. Blend well. Add enough light ale to make a batter the consistency of thick cream. Strain into a clean basin.

Heat the fat in a deep pan. Pass the bananas through the batter and deep fry until crisp and brown. Drain well and cover with sifted icing sugar. Serve at once. (The batter can be made ahead of time, but the cooking must be done at the last moment.)

Shopping List

2 lb minced beef
1 green pepper
3 lb potatoes
12 bananas
1 onion
4 oz liver pâté

Dried tarragon
1 medium tin tomatoes
1 lb lard
Corn meal
1 can light ale
Madeira

BASIC RECIPES

French Dressing

1 teaspoon salt
½ teaspoon black pepper
½ teaspoon Dijon mustard

2 tablespoons wine vinegar
10 tablespoons oil

Blend together the salt, pepper, and mustard. Stir in the vinegar and then the oil. This is enough for about four salads. I usually keep it in a small jar and draw on it when I need it.

If you want it thickened, take out the required amount, put it in a cup and add 1 ice cube; stir gently with a teaspoon for a couple of minutes, take out the ice cube and use at once.

Sweet French Dressing

1 teaspoon salt
2 teaspoons caster sugar
½ teaspoon dry mustard
2 tablespoons wine vinegar

½ teaspoon black pepper
½ teaspoon Dijon mustard
2 teaspoons A.I. Sauce
8 tablespoons oil

Blend together the salt, pepper, sugar, mustard, and the A.I. sauce. Add the oil gradually, stirring all the time. When it is thick and smooth stir in the vinegar.

This will also keep in a jar for use as required.

137

Mayonnaise

2 egg yolks
½ teaspoon black pepper
½ pt oil

1 teaspoon salt
1 tablespoon wine vinegar

Put the egg yolks into a bowl with the salt and pepper. Stir steadily until it is well blended and the yolks have started to get thick and shiny. Start adding the oil very slowly, drop by drop, stirring all the time. It should start to thicken almost at once. When you have added about half the oil, stir in the vinegar. Then continue with the oil, pouring it in a thin stream as there is less danger of it curdling once the vinegar has been added. When all the oil has been added you should have a thick jelly-like sauce.

If you are going to keep it in the fridge for a while before using it, stir in a tablespoon of boiling water. This will stop it separating.

If you like a sauce with a bit of a kick to it stir in either a teaspoon of Dijon mustard or ½ teaspoon of dry mustard, at the beginning.

For *Sauce Mousseline* fold in ¼ pt whipped cream at the end (this is delicious with fish or asparagus).

For *Sauce Tartare* stir 2 tablespoons chopped capers, 2 tablespoons finely chopped gherkins and 1 tablespoon of chopped parsley at the end.

| *Béchamel or* | 2 oz butter | 2 oz flour |
| *White Sauce* | 1 pt milk | Salt, pepper, nutmeg |

Melt the butter gently in a small saucepan and stir in the flour, blending well. Cook over a gentle heat, stirring constantly, until the mixture forms a ball and leaves the sides of the pan. Start adding the warmed milk gradually, stirring well between each addition but allowing the liquid to come to the boil in the pan before you start to stir it. When all the milk has been added, simmer gently for a few minutes more, then stir in the seasoning. This can either be set aside for later use, or even stored in a bowl in the fridge if it is covered with a wetted disc of greaseproof paper which has been cut to fit the diameter of the bowl or saucepan exactly.

This makes a sauce of a good pouring consistency, but where a sauce of a thicker or thinner consistency is required the quantities have been adjusted accordingly (or nutmeg omitted) in individual recipes.

| *Vanilla Sugar* | 1 lb of caster sugar | 1 vanilla bean |

Pour the sugar into a jar with an air-tight lid, bury the bean in it, and cover securely.

Each time you use some of the vanilla sugar just top it up with more caster sugar. As long as you leave it for 24 hours between each topping up the sugar will have a strong, true vanilla flavour. I find that the beans lose their strength and have to be replaced about every six months.

GLOSSARY OF COOKING TERMS AND UNUSUAL COOKING IMPLEMENTS USED IN THIS BOOK

(1) BAKE BLIND
This phrase refers to flan cases made of pastry. The method is as follows: Grease the tin or flan ring lightly with butter, roll out the pastry, and ease it gently into the tin being careful not to stretch it. Cut off the edge neatly. Put a circle of greaseproof paper on to the pastry and fill with either rice or dried beans and bake. The rice or beans which have been used for the purpose cannot, of course, be eaten but the same beans can be kept in a jar and used over and over again. I have been using the same lot for about five years.

(2) CARAMELIZE
This is the process of cooking sugar until it becomes a deep golden brown. It is either cooked in a saucepan with water or sprinkled on the top of a pudding and put under a hot grill until it melts and bubbles. In either case great care must be taken not to let it burn or blacken as it will then taste bitter and nasty.

(3) GARLIC PRESS
This is a small metal implement which can be bought from any good kitchen suppliers or large store. If you are going to cook with garlic frequently it is invaluable as you can get every scrap of flavour out of the garlic without having to eat it in pieces which can be disagreeable.

(4) MANDOLINE
This can also be bought from the same kind of shops as the garlic press. It is sometimes called a Universal Slicer. It consists of a piece of wood with sharp adjustable blades set into it. It is quite invaluable for fine slicing and cuts faster and thinner than you could ever do by hand, even with a very sharp knife.

140

(5) PESTLE AND MORTAR

This is a heavy bowl with a lip and an equally heavy plunger with a rounded end. The purpose is to crush food into a fine paste, and pulping in any other way never makes it quite so smooth.

(6) SCALD

To bring liquids just to boiling point without quite allowing them to boil.

(7) SWEAT

The process of cooking vegetables in butter gently in a covered pan for about 5–10 minutes without letting them brown.

INDEX

Index

References are to page numbers not to menus

A

APPLES
Apples, Baked, 119
Apple Cake, 97
Apple Charlotte, 43
Apple Crumble, 133
Apple Flan, 64
Apple Flan, Crispy, 107
Apples, Jellied, 33
Apple Soufflé, Caramelized, 24
APRICOTS
Apricots, Baked, 66
Apricot Fool, 118
Artichokes Vinaigrette, 13
ASPARAGUS
Asparagus, 18
Asparagus Salad, 79
Assiette Anglaise, 42
Aubergines au Gratin, 77
Avocado Vinaigrette, 27

B

Bake Blind, 140
BANANAS
Bananas with Rum, Baked, 121
Banana Fritters, 136
Banana Meringue, 35
BEANS
Beans, Flageolet, 52
Beans, French, 17
Béchamel or White Sauce, 139
BEEF
Bœuf Bourguignonne, 56
Bœuf en Croûte, 70
Chili con Carne, 1
Entrecôte Steaks Béarnaise, 79
Fillet of Beef with Tomato Fondue, 109

Roast Beef, Cold, 39
Steak Tartare, 37
Blackcurrant Ice Cream, 94
Brandied Crème Brûlée, 49

C

Camembert Cheese and Pears, 131
Caramelize, 140
Carrot Salad, 55
Cauliflower Vinaigrette, 67
Celeriac Remoulade, 108
Charentais Melons with Port, 10
Cheese Soufflés, 52
Cherry Almond Pudding, 123
CHICKEN
Chickens with Almonds, Baby, 30
Chicken Croquettes, 34
Chicken Curry, 13
Chicken with Aspic, Cold, 95
Chicken with Herbs, 106
Chicken Liver Pâté, 21
Chicken Souvaroff, 68
Chicken with Tarragon, 45
CHICORY
Braised Chicory, 118
Chicory and Beetroot Salad, 7
Chicory Salad, 54
Chili con Carne, 1
CHOCOLATE
Chocolate Fudge Pudding, 114
Chocolat, Pot, 57
Coffee Soufflé, 26
Cole Slaw, 64
Consommé, 5
CRAB
Crab and Celeriac Salad, 47
Crab, Devilled, 70
Crab Soufflé, 21

Crème Caramel, 111
Crunchy Flapjacks, 88
Cucumber Salad, 19

D

DESSERTS
  Apple Cake, 97
  Apple Charlotte, 43
  Apple Crumble, 133
  Apple Flan, 64
  Apricot Fool, 118
  Baked Apricots, 66
  Baked Apples, 119
  Baked Bananas with Rum, 121
  Baked Peaches, 99
  Banana Fritters, 136
  Banana Meringue, 35
  Blackcurrant Ice Cream, 94
  Brandied Crème Brûlée, 49
  Camembert Cheese and Pears, 131
  Cherry Almond Pudding, 123
  Chocolate Fudge Pudding, 114
  Crème Caramel, 111
  Crispy Apple Flan, 107
  Crunchy Flapjacks, 88
  Coffee Soufflé, 26
  French Saucer Pancakes, 96
  Fresh Peaches, 85
  Gâteau de Riz, 116
  Grand Marnier Ice Cream, 72
  Honey Cream, 78
  Hot Caramelized Apple Soufflé, 24
  Iced Lemon Soufflé, 59
  Iced Zabaglione, 7
  Jellied Apples, 33
  Lemon Ice Cream, 11
  Meringues with Walnuts, 84
  Orange Chiffon, 31
  Orange and Kirsch Soufflés, 129
  Orange Salad with Almonds, 126
  Orange Salad with Cointreau, 109
  Peach Soufflé, 69
  Pears Melba, 62
  Pêche Brûlée, 28
  Pêche Cœur à la Crème, 102
  Pineapple with Kirsch, 51
  Poached Oranges with Cointreau, 46

  Pot Chocolat, 57
  Raspberry Meringue Tarts, 92
  Raspberry Mille Feuilles, 22
  Raspberries and Redcurrants, 17
  Raspberry Trifle, 81
  Strawberries and Cream, 90
  Strawberries Romanoff, 20
  Strawberry Delight, 15
  Strawberry Flan, 75
  Summer Pudding, 40
  Syllabub, 54
  Treacle Tart, 104
  Vanilla Soufflé with Strawberries, 38
Ducklings, Roast, 47

E

EGGS
  Egg Mayonnaise, 56
  Eggs Mimosa, 25
  Hash with Eggs, 123
  Piperade, 39
  Spanish Potato Omelette, 131
Escalope de Veau Viennoise, 16
Escalopes of Veal à la Crème, 74
Escargots, 44
Exotic Meatballs, 135

F

FISH AND SHELLFISH
  Buttered Shrimps, 115
  Crab and Celeriac Salad, 47
  Crab Soufflé, 21
  Creamed Prawns and Rice, 127
  Devilled Crab, 70
  Fish Ritz, 61
  Iced Salmon Mousse and Cucumber, 1
  Ostende Tomatoes, 97
  Poached Salmon, 19
  Prawn Risotto, 93
  Salmon Mousse, 63
  Salmon Pudding, 119
  Salmon Trout and Cucumber, 23
  Shrimp Fritters, 91
  Smoked Haddock Soufflé, 101

Sole Florentine, 87
Tarama Salata, 32
Tunny Fish with Onion, 67
Turbot Provençal, 50
Vol-au-vent Fruits du Mer, 5
Flageolet Beans, 59
French Beans, 17
French Dressing, 137
French Dressing, Sweet, 137
Fruit Mayonnaise, 83

G

Garlic Press, 140
Gâteau de Riz, 116
Grand Marnier Ice Cream, 72
Green Salad with Avocado, 89

H

Haddock Soufflé, Smoked, 101
HAM
Ham and Cheese Tart, 99
Ham and Chicory, Creamed, 133
Ham in Cream Sauce, 32
Ham Pancakes, 121
Ham Pastries, 89
Ham and Salami, Cold, 77
Hash with Eggs, 123
Honey Cream, 78

HORS D'ŒUVRE (COLD)
Artichokes Vinaigrette, 13
Asparagus Salad, 79
Avocado Vinaigrette, 27
Carrot Salad, 55
Cauliflower Vinaigrette, 67
Celeriac Remoulade, 108
Charentais Melons with Port, 10
Chicken Liver Pâté, 21
Crab and Celeriac Salad, 47
Cucumber Salad, 108
Egg Mayonnaise, 56
Egg Mimosa, 25
Fruit Mayonnaise, 83
Lentil Salad, 82
Melon and Parma Ham, 23
Pâté Maison, 50
Ratatouille en Salade, 16
Salade Creole, 113

Salade Niçoise, 110
Salmon Mousse, 63
Tarama Salata, 32
Tomato Salad, 55
Tunny Fish and Onion, 67
Tunny Fish and Tomato Salad, 117
HORS D'ŒUVRE (HOT)
Asparagus, 18
Aubergines au Gratin, 77
Devilled Crab, 70
Escargots, 44
Individual Cheese Soufflés, 52
Piperade, 39
Tomatoes in Cream, 65

I

ICE CREAM
Blackcurrant, 94
Grand Marnier, 72
Lemon, 11

K

KIDNEYS
Kidneys Richard, 87
Sautéd Kidneys with Boiled Rice, 25

L

LAMB
Double Lamb Cutlets, 83
Lamb Cutlets, 63
Racks of Lamb, 117
Roast Lamb with Garlic, 58
Leek and Potato Soup, 58
Lemon Ice Cream, 11
Lemon Soufflé, Iced, 59
Lettuce and Cucumber Salad, 11
Liver with Courgettes, Calves, 113

M

Mandoline or Universal Slicer, 140
Mayonnaise, 138
MEATS
Assiette Anglaise, 42
Bœuf Bourguignonne, 56
Bœuf en Croûte, 70

Calves Liver with Courgettes, 113
Chili con Carne, 1
Cold Ham and Salami, 77
Cold Roast Beef, 39
Creamed Ham and Chicory, 133
Double Lamb Cutlets, 83
Entrecôte Steaks Béarnaise, 79
Escalope de Veau Viennoise, 16
Fillet of Beef with Tomato
    Fondue, 109
Ham in Cream Sauce, 32
Ham Pastries, 89
Kidneys Richard, 87
Lamb Cutlets, 63
Meatballs, 135
Moussaka, 125
Occo Bucco, 52
Pork Chops, 115
Raçitura, 103
Racks of Lamb, 117
Roast Lamb with Garlic, 58
Roast Loin of Pork with Wine
    Gravy, 65
Sautéd Kidneys and Rice, 25
Steak Tartare, 37
Veal Chops with Tarragon, 27
Veal Escalopes à la Crème, 74
Veal Maison, 110
Melon with Port, Charentais, 10
Melon and Parma Ham, 23
Meringues with Walnuts, 84
Minestrone Soup, 42
Mocha, 4
Mostarda de Cremona, 78

N

Noodles, 75

O

Omelette, Spanish Potato, 131
ORANGES
Orange Chiffon, 31
Orange and Kirsch Soufflé, 129
Oranges with Cointreau, Poached,
    46
Orange Salad, 49

Orange Salad with Almonds, 126
Orange Salad with Cointreau, 109
Osso Bucco, 52
Ostende Tomatoes, 97

P

Pancakes, French Saucer, 96
Pancakes, Ham, 121
Pâté, Chicken Liver, 21
Pâté Maison, 50
PEACHES
Baked Peaches, 99
Fresh Peaches, 85
Peach Soufflé, 69
Pêche Brûlée, 28
Pêche Cœur à la Crème, 102
Pears Melba, 62
Peas, 19
Pea Soup, 37
Peppers au Gratin, 115
Pestle and Mortar, 141
Petits Pois, 111
Pineapple with Kirsch, 51
Piperade, 39
Pork Chops, 115
Pork Loin with Wine Gravy, 65
POTATOES
Crusty Potato Bake, 114
French Fried Potatoes, 80
Jacket Potatoes, 43
New Potatoes, 19
Pommes de Terre au Beurre, 71
Potatoes with Cream, 45
Potato Salad, 23
Purée Potatoes, 7
Roast Potatoes, 48
Sauté Potatoes, 17
Steamed Potatoes, 51
POULTRY
Baby Chickens with Almonds, 30
Chicken Croquettes, 34
Chicken with Herbs, 106
Chicken Souvaroff, 68
Chicken with Tarragon, 45
Cold Chicken with Aspic, 95
Mild Chicken Curry, 13
Risotto al Pollo, 10
Roast Ducklings, 47

Roast Turkey with Chestnut
Stuffing, 6
Prawns and Rice, Creamed, 127
Prawn Risotto, 93

R

Raçitura, 103
RASPBERRIES
Raspberries and Redcurrants, 17
Raspberry Meringue Tarts, 92
Raspberry Mille Feuilles, 22
Raspberry Trifle, 81
Ratatouille en Salade, 16
RICE DISHES
Prawn Risotto, 93
Rice, Boiled, 14
Rice Salad, 95
Rice Pizza, 129
Risotto al Pollo, 10
Risotto Milanese, 53
Russian Salad, 39

S

SALADS
Asparagus, 79
Carrot, 55
Cauliflower Vinaigrette, 67
Celeriac Remoulade, 108
Chicory, 54
Chicory and Beetroot, 7
Cole Slaw, 64
Creole, 113
Cucumber, 19
Green with Avocado, 89
Lentil, 82
Lettuce and Cucumber, 11
Niçoise, 110
Orange, 49
Potato, 23
Ratatouille, 16
Rice, 95
Russian, 39
Tomato, 55
Tomato and Cucumber, 75
Tomato and Onion, 91
Tomato and Pepper, 33
Tunny Fish and Tomato, 117

SALMON
Iced Salmon Mousse and
Cucumber, 1
Poached Salmon, 19
Salmon Mousse, 63
Salmon Pudding, 119
Salmon Trout and Cucumber, 23
Salsify Provençal, 28
Scald, 141
Shrimps, Buttered, 115
Shrimp Fritters, 91
Sole Florentine, 85
SOUFFLÉS (SAVOURY)
Cheese, 52
Crab, 21
Smoked Haddock, 101
SOUFFLÉS (SWEET)
Apple, Hot Caramelized, 24
Coffee, 26
Lemon, 59
Orange and Kirsch, 129
Peach, 69
Vanilla with Strawberries, 38
SOUPS
Consommé, 5
Leek and Potato, 58
Minestrone, 42
Pea, 37
Perisioare, 60
Tomato Consommé, Iced, 74
Vichyssoise, 30
Watercress and Potato, Iced, 34
Spinach, Leaf, 35
Steak Tartare, 37
STRAWBERRIES
Strawberries and Cream, 90
Strawberries Romanoff, 20
Strawberry Delight, 15
Strawberry Flan, 75
Summer Pudding, 40
Sweat, 141
Syllabub, 54

T

Tarama Salata, 32
TOMATOES
Ostende Tomatoes, 97
Stuffed Tomatoes, 81

Tomato Consommé, Iced, 74
Tomatoes in Cream, 65
Tomato and Cucumber Salad, 75
Tomato and Onion Salad, 91
Tomato and Pepper Salad, 33
Tomato Salad, 55
Treacle Tart, 104
Tunny Fish with Onion, 67
Tunny Fish and Tomato Salad, 117
Turbot Provençal, 50
Turkey and Chestnut Stuffing, 6

V

VEAL
Escalope de Veau Viennoise, 16
Osso Bucco, 52
Veal Chops with Tarragon, 27
Veal Escalopes à la Crème, 74
Veal Maison, 110
Vanilla Sugar, 139
Vanilla Soufflé with Strawberries, 38

VEGETABLES
Asparagus, 18
Aubergines au Gratin, 77
Braised Chicory, 118
Flageolet Beans, 59
French Beans, 17
Leaf Spinach, 35
Peas, 19
Petits Pois, 111
Peppers au Gratin, 115
Salsify Provençal, 28
Stuffed Tomatoes, 81
Vichyssoise, 30
Vol-au-vent Fruits du Mer, 5

W

Watercress and Potato Soup, 34

Z

Zabaglione, Iced, 7